Meditations in Wonderland

ANNA PATRICK

RIVER GROVE
BOOKS

*For the brave, curious, and hungry souls
who have ever fallen down the rabbit hole.*

*And for Mom, Dad, and Cezar,
as well as my late Nana and Papa,
who have always encouraged me to do so.*

Published by River Grove Books
Austin, TX
www.rivergrovebooks.com

Distributed by River Grove Books

For ordering information or special discounts for bulk purchases, please contact River Grove Books at PO Box 91869, Austin, TX 78709, 512.891.6100.

Design and composition by Greenleaf Book Group and Kim Lance
Cover design by Greenleaf Book Group and Kim Lance
Cover image (small girl):©iStockphoto.com/myillo

Cataloging in Publication Data is available.

ISBN: 978-1-63299-045-7

First Edition

Other Edition(s):
eBook ISBN: 978-1-63299-046-4

WE SHALL NOT CEASE FROM EXPLORATION,

AND AT THE END OF ALL OF OUR EXPLORING

WE WILL FIND THAT WE

HAVE ARRIVED WHERE WE STARTED,

AND THAT WE NOW KNOW

THE PLACE FOR THE FIRST TIME.

—T. S. ELIOT

One

&lizabeth stumbled into the bathroom and groped the wall
for the light switch with the needy fingers of someone func-
tioning from the blurred state between being awake and being
asleep, where the subconscious mind still pulls the strings.

The light streaming in from the window behind her caught
the medicine cabinet mirror, beckoning her. She flicked the
light on and rubbed her temples as she approached the sink.
She didn't reach for her toothbrush. Instead, she gripped the
sides of the sink, her white knuckles complementing the porcelain, as she held in a scream. It wasn't the toothbrush she
was after this morning.

"Almost there," Elizabeth murmured, as she came closer
and closer to catching her own gaze in the mirror. Invisible
needles pricked her spine as eye contact became more immi-
nent, making her damp grip slide on the porcelain. Slowly,
slowly, her eyes inched upward to meet themselves in her
reflection.

When her gaze finally connected in the mirror, she thought
her eyes looked like black holes, despite the fact that they were
really a dark shade of green. To her they looked like a doll's
eyes, as if behind their luster resided secrets long withheld,
locked away beneath their glassy depths, entombed in a place

few dared to reach. She noticed the wrinkles on her forehead and the faded acne scars. She observed the thin, white scar above her left eye, where her childhood cat scratched her long ago. She saw the delicate skin under her eyes as an abyss of purple, twisted veins. The sight of her canvas of skin and sunken eyes caused her to furrow her brow, which only made the story lines on her face grow deeper. They began to look like trenches, and when Elizabeth tugged at them they fell back into place like obedient soldiers. As she stood there an acidic revulsion crawled through her, and made the hairs on the back of her neck stand at attention.

She looked away, and the goose bumps that dotted her neck subsided, leaving her body cold. She picked up her toothbrush and threw it at the sink, hard, as if she wanted it to fly down the drain and reappear in another dimension.

"Ellie? You alright in there?" said her boyfriend, Adam, who sat with Fitz, their French bulldog, just feet away on the living room couch.

"Yeah, I'm fine," she called out to him, her pulse racing. "I just dropped something." It was on days like this that the studio apartment she and Adam shared took the form of a small labyrinth, with each sound reverberating against the maze of walls, closing in on them in a broken chorus. She unwrapped her fingers from the sink and splashed cold water on her face.

What's wrong with you! her internal monologue began. *Who can't look at themselves in the mirror? Are you crazy?*

"Enough!" Elizabeth whispered, "Not today."

The cold water did nothing but awaken her to the realization that her pills were inside the medicine cabinet, just within her reach, concealed within a small pouch hidden behind her perfume bottle so that Adam would never find them. The thought of them made the clamor of her inner chorus grow quiet.

Her fingers fumbled the creaky mirror open, revealing the medicine cabinet's innards—the bathroom secrets kept tucked away from prying eyes: the embarrassing creams, the "feminine products," the prescribed topicals with faded labels, and Elizabeth's black velvet pouch that contained blue and orange pills.

Blue or orange day?

She had to be quick. She had two, maybe three, minutes until Adam would knock to check on her. The *10* stamped on the blue pills looked less appealing than the *20* printed on the orange one, but to her disappointment, there were only three left. They looked like candy in her glistening palm.

Guess it's time to call Mack, she mused, as an image of her drug dealer swept through her mind. She found a sad sense of comfort at the thought of his outstretched hand holding a fifty-dollar bag of uppers. She met Mack in college and was fairly certain that Adam had no idea he existed. It was a coincidental stroke of luck that Mack came back to live in Brooklyn with his parents, just a few blocks away from where she now stood. Elizabeth had his number saved in her phone under "Mom's Office." The memory of his hands danced through her mind, unmoved by protest or better judgment. She longed to feel the bag transferring to her own hands, the crinkling of the paper she shoved back into his, followed by the flash of the blue butterfly tattoo on his right wrist before he faded back into the darkness from whence he came. And then she would leave and pretend it never happened.

Orange day.

She quickly popped the pill with *20* stamped on the front into her mouth with her shaking hands and swallowed it dry.

Nothing serious. Just for recreation.

Just for recreation. Helps me focus, that's all.

I am strong. I am strong and in control.

She heard the teapot scream from the kitchen area, which was only a few feet away thanks to the tactical layout of their studio apartment, followed by Adam's hurried footsteps as he rushed to take it off the stove. For a moment, she thought he might hand deliver her cup.

Oh, God. Don't come in here, she pleaded, as she felt her heartbeat in her palms. She held the pouch behind her back and faced the door. She heard the cup clink on the table in the living room.

That was close, she thought, *but, if it's not a big deal, why not tell him?*

Better yet, why not try an honest look in the mirror?

She put the pouch back quietly. The relentless buzzing of accusations and questions in her head abated until they were nothing more than a murmur. She leaned her forehead against the glass and released a tense breath.

Maybe tomorrow. Tomorrow I'll look in that mirror and hold that gaze. I'll see my real self, Elizabeth thought, as she did almost everyday.

She made herself that promise most mornings. It became nearly as routine as brushing her teeth. After Elizabeth parted from her sheets, as the sun rose and the world began to stir, she would lose herself in her morning rituals: sliding on her slippers, drowsily brewing her tea, combing her hair with her fingers, and brushing her teeth as she meandered around the kitchen lost in thought. But on this particular morning, Elizabeth remained in the bathroom and stared into the abyss, trying once more to find the light in the darkness behind her eyes, and it kept her from her tea.

Finally, she emerged with sunken shoulders and a quiet mind.

"Ellie?" Adam asked again.

"What?" she asked, with a bright smile.

"You sound cheery."

"Of course!" she smiled, "Why wouldn't I be? I—"

She backed into the living room chair, knocking her worn, black leather purse to the floor. A white compact with pink borders stamped decoratively along its sides tumbled out with the other forgotten objects. She didn't open it to check if it had broken. But rather, she stuffed it at the bottom of the bag with the rest of her neglected treasures, which she picked up from the scratched wood floor: the crumpled-up to-do lists and grocery lists, a lipstick, a mascara, and a notebook for writing down the fleeting thoughts she didn't want to forget.

She dropped the bag back on the chair, where it landed with a thud. Then she turned and faced her old wooden armoire. From its contents, she chose a soft, red cotton tank top and tight, black, leather leggings, with back pockets that were stitched with a tribal pattern. They felt like a second skin.

From the living room sofa, Fitz left Adam's side to trot

loyally behind Elizabeth. He jumped down from the couch, onto the old Persian carpet that Elizabeth's mother gave her and Adam as a housewarming gift, and landed heavily on the floor. As he ran past the small dining table in front of the couch, he leapt over one of its legs, causing the table to shake and almost topple the picture frame resting on top of it. The frame held one of Elizabeth's favorite photos of her and Adam, which captured them together at the beach they visited last summer. Their eyes shone like the green sea foam that encircled their ankles. It was one of many photographs of the two of them that littered the apartment. On their kitchen counter sat a picture of them wearing long black gowns, their college diplomas clutched in their fists like trophies. The picture next to it captured them dancing the night away at a family party a few months prior, with Adam spinning Elizabeth, who had kicked off her heels. Their desk sat across the small room, and on it rested an old photograph of them at their senior prom. It was the only photograph that documented the first few years of their relationship. A film of dust speckled the glass frame. Elizabeth always told herself she would wipe it off but never did.

Then there was the collage that Elizabeth put together one rainy day, though she claimed it was never quite finished. It was almost entirely black and white. There were three small photographs of her and Adam at various celebrations, and two more of them with both sets of parents. The one picture printed in full color dominated the collage, even though it was nestled at the bottom. From the bottom left-hand corner, an old photo of Elizabeth's favorite childhood pet, a red-orange tabby cat named Lucifer, grinned a toothy grin.

From the kitchen, Elizabeth snapped out of her trance for a moment. Fitz nearly bumped into the back of her legs as he skidded to a stop. She looked over at Adam, with his curly black hair still messily pushed to one side from sleep, while his lush green eyes stared back at her with that look that gave her those familiar butterflies. His eyes were green, like the forests she longed to get lost in. She knew his eyes better than her own, and her anxiety dissipated as soon as she caught his gaze. He was handsome, in a careless way, like he had no idea what he looked like most of the time. His smile had a tinge of arrogance to it—the kind of smile that only boys who have been handsome from a young age possess. He didn't take his eyes off of her.

"What are you looking at?"

"You," he grinned.

"Like what you see?" she smirked.

"I'm wondering what it is *you* see."

"What do you mean? I just—"

"Just see me. I know," he said. "I mean I'm wondering how you see yourself."

Elizabeth clenched her jaw.

"It didn't sound like you dropped something in there," he said with a pause, "It sounded like you threw something. Did that have something to do with looking in the mirror?"

She relaxed her jaw as the orange pill brought her back to life, leaving her with an acidic aftertaste and a quiet mind.

"You're my mirror," she said with a smile. "You should know that by now."

He held her gaze. It occurred to her that he really was a reflection of herself, her own ideal image printed backward.

She knew it from the day she met him, when they were teenagers. He had given her butterflies ever since—the old friends that fluttered in her stomach now, dancing their usual dance.

Their love matured along with them as they navigated their college years. After graduation they moved in together, adopted Fitz, and built a home that reflected the home in their hearts in which the other dwelled. Their differences complemented one another to create a symmetrical balance, and through their openness and honesty, they could point out strengths and weaknesses in one another that, like a cancer, could otherwise remain unseen to the infected. On the first night they spent together in their apartment they vowed to treat their relationship like a spiritual practice. A spiritual practice meant dedication and bringing awareness to each moment, which Elizabeth struggled with on this particular morning. But Adam's fascination with her did not falter, even on mornings like these.

Candles were always lit, and dust was swept under the rug, where it accumulated slowly over their years together. When clutter piled up, it mounted in designated places. A stack of unpaid bills towered high on the kitchen counter, and old cooking magazines that Elizabeth had never opened sat on the counter, surrounded by chipped paint. But it was their clutter, and Elizabeth and Adam grew to love it over the years.

"You didn't answer my question," Adam interjected after a minute of silence.

"Well, I—"

Before Elizabeth could answer, she tripped over a pair of Adam's worn, light blue sneakers, which somehow always managed to be in the way.

"Sorry, I was going to put those away—"

"No, it's fine," she stammered, happy to be let off the hook. "You always know how to keep me on my toes."

She had even grown to love Adam's contribution to the clutter, including the light blue sneakers that Adam always wore, despite the fact that Elizabeth had bought him a new pair for his twenty-fourth birthday last year. He remained loyal to them, despite the holes and frayed edges. Elizabeth began to overlook the initial annoyance she felt at the rejection of the new shoes as time went by, and she accepted his old, beat-up pair as a fixture in their apartment. She had carefully moved them away from Fitz's wandering eye during his teething phase. Sometimes, she even cleaned the scuffs off their soles, and though Adam didn't always know how to thank her outright, he would take great care to give extra compliments on the dinner she made, or on the way she wore her hair. Over time, Elizabeth recognized this pattern in him, and if any moments of tension arose, she would remember his subtle appreciation for her, even as she caught sight of the sneakers lying in their usual spot, right in her way.

"Want a quick breakfast?" he asked quietly.

"Breakfast? You haven't cooked breakfast since we moved in together," she grinned. "And anyway, I think I'm going to get a quick meditation in before work."

She walked toward him and wrapped her fingers behind his neck, pulling him closer. He smelled like their warm bed linens. Her top lip found the familiar fold between his, and as she kissed him she breathed him in. He leaned into her, grazing the inside of her leg lightly with his fingers, sending a pulse like a sigh through her body. She let her hand slide down his chest and land in his lap. For a moment, she wanted to escape herself and become a part of him.

Fitz let out a bark, releasing them from the moment. He pawed the couch, wanting to be scooped up and placed at Adam's side, where he expected to remain until Elizabeth left for work. She and Adam both worked in the city, commuting at the usual hours. He worked as an actor, and she worked as an interior designer. Though at times their lifestyle felt like a revolving door of feast and famine, the artists inside them never slept.

"Sounds great," he whispered as he leaned back and put his hands behind his head like a king, the veins in his forearms standing at attention. Sometimes they meditated together, holding hands and synchronizing their breaths. To them, it felt more intimate than sex.

"It won't be long. Ten minutes? I have to leave for work soon, anyway."

"Sure. What music do you want today? Bach? Nature sounds? Anything but the whales again."

"No sound today," she smiled back. "I'm enjoying the quiet."

Elizabeth left Adam and Fitz and sauntered over to the small corner of the room by the window that they had turned into a cozy meditation space. She placed a miniature statue of Buddha on a small side table in front of the window, with a desk clock resting at his side. In front of the Buddha, there was a pink yoga mat, rolled out and welcoming. Several shelves hung on the wall on either side of the window, which housed assorted objects from their childhood, collecting dust: Adam's forgotten soccer trophies, the old prom picture in its dusty black frame that showcased two young faces that have since turned older, and the collage with Lucifer's wide, fanged grin staring back at her. The last object on the shelf was Elizabeth's favorite: a small *Alice in Wonderland* doll that she favored throughout her youth, whose hair was in a perpetual state of unkempt from playtimes past. The doll's familiar blue dress had faded over the years, but Elizabeth could never seem to put her away for good. During their move, she had held her over a box with "for charity" scribbled sloppily across the side, staring deeply into her old blue eyes, but she couldn't part with the doll. Instead, she turned and put her back on the shelf, where she still sat, her frozen gaze exuding an elixir of truth.

After a few seconds, Elizabeth looked away from Alice, returning to the ambience of her meditation corner. Compared to the chaos and clutter, this corner was always clean. She felt this corner was awake, wielding its own energy that surged outward and emanated through the rest of their space. She began to prepare for her meditation, setting her meditation timer, turning the desk clock on its face, so she wouldn't be distracted by the time, and brushing off the yoga mat on which she sat on the hardwood floor.

Then she heard Adam's soft footsteps, followed by Fitz's smaller ones, approaching quietly behind her.

Adam stopped right behind her, kneeling down to where she sat on the yoga mat. As Fitz lay down underneath the Buddha's table, Adam kissed the top of Elizabeth's head and then dropped to his knees. He ran his fingers through her long, black hair and pushed it over one shoulder, lightly tracing his fingertips over her neck, which shot little electric pulses down her body like lightning. The butterflies in her stomach stirred all at once. She turned around to face him.

"Can I ask you something?"

"Make it quick," she sighed.

"Why is it that you never really look at yourself in the mirror?"

"What are you talking about?"

"You avoided my question when I tried to ask you about it earlier."

"I wasn't avoiding the question. I just got distracted," she fired back.

Fitz perked his ears forward from where he sprawled underneath the Buddha, unsure of his role in the discussion. For a moment all that could be heard were the phantom steps of the person living in the apartment above.

"I know what I heard, Ellie. I know you threw something in the bathroom this morning, even though you lied about it twice. So, I just wanted to say . . . I just want you to know . . . that I think you're beautiful, and I hope you see that when you look in the mirror. That's all."

"That's not all," she said. "Say what you mean!"

"I'm sayin—"

"I don't have a self-esteem problem, Adam. If anything, I can be a bit vain, just like you."

"You don't think it's a little . . . off?"

"*Off*? No, it's just a routine. I do it when I'm half-asleep! I could ask you why you insist on leaving your sneakers in the middle of the floor, but I don't. It's just a quirk of yours, just like this is just a little quirk of mine. Can we just leave it at that?" Elizabeth felt her face grow hot. Fitz shifted his gaze as she clenched her jaw and lightly wiped her palms on the side of her thighs.

"Do you not like what you see?" he insisted, after a minute of silence. His words reverberated off the walls, like the sound of the flying toothbrush earlier, shooting back at her from all directions.

"I have no problem facing myself," she said after a pause, "But when I look at you right now, I'm not sure you can say the same."

Adam's eyes widened.

"I'm serious, Adam. Would you like to see yourself right now? The way you're judging and ambushing me!"

"Judging you? Christ, I just—"

"No, it's not 'just.' I don't appreciate your moral righteousness, and I'm not going to let you tell me how I feel!"

"That's not what I was trying to do," he said as he threw up his hands. "I'm sorry if it came off that way."

"Spare me the self-confidence pep talk, Adam," she said. "I don't have time for this little intervention. I know you know me better than this. Even if I wanted to entertain this conversation, now just isn't a good time."

"Alright, fine," he caved, looking like a snake had just bitten him. "I just wanted to reflect on something I saw this morning. I'm your mirror, right?"

"Right," she said, as she let her jaw relax. She put her hand on his knee, drawing little circles with her fingertips. He put his hand over hers, damp but strong.

"I just want you to know that I love you, and I think you're beautiful. I just want you to let that sink in."

Sitting face to face with Adam on the yoga mat, Elizabeth interpreted the look in his eyes to mean that he still clung to his theories on her intimate inner workings, much of which were still unexplored territory for her.

"Adam, I'm fine, really," she pleaded, half for him to believe her and half for wanting him to leave her in peace.

He took her hand in his and squeezed her palm. "You know, you can tell me anything," he said in a whisper. "You can tell me what you see."

"Right now I just see you."

He smiled. "I'll leave you to your meditation then," he said. "But I want to talk about this later."

"Fine. We can talk about it later, if there's anything more to say."

"You sure you don't want me to play some Bach for you on my laptop?"

"No. Just silence, please."

Adam let out an exasperated sigh as he got up and disappeared into the kitchen. Fitz lingered for a moment but came when Adam called him, leaving Elizabeth to herself in the corner of the room.

As she smoothed out wrinkle after wrinkle on her yoga mat, the uneasiness she experienced in front of the mirror began to return to her, steadily rising to the surface at a pace that frightened her.

What was that? she asked herself. *I snapped at him. Where the hell did that come from?*

Adam shuffled about in the kitchen, with Fitz, a few feet away from her, clinking glasses together as he poured himself his morning orange juice, but the sound never reached her ears. Adam and Fitz seemed to be in a separate world, far away from where she now sat, suddenly uneager to begin her meditation.

What if he's right?

Her jaw clenched again, as her morning began to replay in her mind. The discomfort she felt when she looked in the mirror was chronic to the point that she hardly noticed it anymore. Instead, she treated it like you would an old injury, mindlessly avoiding putting pressure on it. It always started with that familiar tension, right after she flipped on the light. Then with one pill, on those particularly long mornings, she could focus, and all of her doubts and worries would disappear. She thought the discomfort had to come from somewhere unchartered within her.

But where?

Who cares? I told him that I can confront myself, she reasoned silently, as if she were having an argument with two sides of herself. Her inner chorus returned, pitting her against herself again. *Enough! I can't meditate like this! The pill can't possibly be wearing off already. Focus and just breathe.*

The only way Elizabeth could collect herself was to focus on her breath, but as she sat to meditate, her conversation with Adam continued to claw its way to the forefront of her mind. She continued to smooth the invisible folds in her yoga mat. She flicked imaginary dust particles off of its surface and bit the inside of her lip.

Is he right? His words flowed through her mind again, loudly at first, and then they quieted down to a whisper, until suddenly it grew quiet in her mind. *Finally!* she thought, *I did take the orange one, after all.*

The silence had the stillness of summer storms, of the moment between thunder and lightning that feels alive with electricity. She channeled the quietness she craved, that she hoped the pill would give her, yet she couldn't shake the deep, resonating feeling that she was not sitting alone.

She turned to face a patch of thick air beside her, finding that the specter of her conversation with Adam still hovered beside her. She felt that the space next to her was heavy, weighed down by the negative energy she had spewed at Adam. She turned to her other side, only to find that that space, too, was occupied. There sat the demon she fought with during each encounter with the mirror. It followed her from room to room, and now it made itself comfortable on her yoga mat.

She turned to look ahead, still biting her lip. In front of her sat two identical, twisted gargoyles of her own unrelenting thoughts. The old gargoyles held hands as if they were twin brothers. She tasted rust as blood seeped from the inside of her lip. Though this was the first time she felt their presence in a tangible form, she recognized their frenzied and staccato energy, as if it were a familiar smile from old friends. She nicknamed them Doubt and Worry. Doubt had a smile frozen in stone across his face, and he covered his eyes with his right hand. Doubt's left hand held Worry's, who sat with a stern expression and widened mouth, etched across his stone surface.

Behind her, she felt the presence of a distinct energy that took a different form than the others, something she could not yet recognize. But when she connected to her breath, the company around her began to fade from her mind, and the air began to clear.

Finally, she took a deep breath into her lower abdomen. Before she closed her eyes to meditate, she quickly glanced at the clock, which was still resting on its face. *Ten minutes*, she told herself, *ten minutes of quiet*.

Then her eyes met those of her orange cat, Lucifer, from his photograph in the collage, followed by the glossy eyes of her Alice doll. Both of them stared back at her from their places on the shelf, waiting for her to close her eyes.

"Here goes nothing," she said, as the world turned to black.

Gone from her vision was the bright apartment that she called home. She felt her stomach rise and fall with each breath, in and out. In and out. Like waves crashing on a war-torn shore. She sat cross-legged with one hand on her lower belly to feel her breath, and one hand on the floor beneath her for grounding. She became engulfed in darkness. Her descent happened slowly at first, but then all at once, much like falling asleep or falling in love.

Suddenly, as she slipped deeper into the abyss of her soul, she saw her own personal rabbit hole unfold before her.

Two

&lizabeth kicked her legs furiously out beneath her, but she
found no floor. The sound of clanging pots in the kitchen
faded away like the sound of the dump trucks that roamed
the streets like prowling panthers in the early morning. The
entire kitchen, with Adam and Fitz in it, evaporated as if they
were the pills on the tip of her tongue. In this new place there
was nothing, except for the lucid consciousness that tugged at
her pant leg and pulled her deeper into the abyss.

She was entombed in darkness, weightless, with no ground
beneath her, yet she continued to descend. She reached out
but found nothing. There was only the sound of her breath to
keep her company during her downward climb. Suddenly, she
began to feel her breath bounce back toward her, as if there
were now a wall on all sides. With each breath, she wound
farther down the dark esophagus of the rabbit hole.

As the tunnel widened, dim shapes took form before her
eyes. She blinked at the interruption of the light in her world
of darkness, an intruder who showed up ten minutes too
late. She had no idea where the light came from, if not from
within her. She began to make out drifting shapes that grew

larger and more detailed as she fell, as if they materialized out of thin air.

But instead of confronting old rocking chairs and ticking clocks on her descent, as she remembered from the childhood story about Alice's rabbit hole, Elizabeth saw Lucifer's red collar, an old tiara she used to play dress up with when she was small, and old love letters from Adam, some torn to shreds and others intact or taped together. The letters bumped into each other, one changing the trajectory of the other. The collar seemed to catch a snag, while the tiara shot across the hole like a shooting star.

Her lipstick and mascara appeared, followed by the compact from her black leather purse, which was just out of her reach. Her shoulder muscles burned as she reached out to touch the mirror. Her long fingers ached to graze its familiar surface, but just as she reached it, her hand slipped through it to the other side. Floating with her was the familiar feeling of having something close by that she couldn't grasp. Instead, it lurked unseen among the bobbing treasures. The rabbit hole became an intoxicating slip into her own darkness, which welcomed her home with open arms.

Suddenly, she heard a voice, softly at first, but then it grew louder from all directions.

"Turn around!"

"Hello?" she called.

More silence.

Turn where? she thought to herself, as she craned her neck, searching for the voice. She saw nothing but empty space both above and below her, which paradoxically felt filled to the brim with something she couldn't describe. The presence commanded the attention of the hairs on the back of her neck.

"Run! Run!" screamed a female voice, as if a dark assailant stood behind her.

She looked over her shoulder once more, only to meet the darkness. Again, there was no one there, only the disembodied voice of an unannounced specter.

Her belongings still hovered around her, like brightly colored fishing lures lying on the surface of calm waters, waiting to attract a bite. For a few minutes, she watched them as they drifted before her like clouds in the sky. Her senses gathered everything all at once—she felt the cold air of the tunnel enclosing around her, and she tasted the moisture oozing off of the mud-like walls, violating her sinuses. In the ringing of her ears she sensed the vibrational ticking of a clock from somewhere far away. She remained connected to her breath, her lifeline in the black seas of the unknown, upon which she floated.

For a moment, she wondered whether this was it for her, whether she would ever reach the bottom, or whether she had come too far and yet not far enough.

"This is the way my life ends," she mused. Cold, detached. *This is the way my life ends,* she thought. *This is the way my life ends, not with a light, but lost in darkness.*

The silent audience of material objects bobbed, nodding in agreement with her thoughts. Each moment died and was reborn in the next, and the ashes that arose were more nothingness, empty and cold, the esophagus of death himself, the sepulchre too heavy for the lid to be lifted.

"Is anyone there? Can anyone hear me?" she said louder, though her voice did not echo.

Then, arising from the abyss, her Alice doll flashed before her, with her perfect blonde hair and blue dress in mint condition. She looked as she did when Elizabeth was a little girl, when she first held her close and told her all her secrets.

"I look nothing like her," Elizabeth mused, with her long, black hair and green eyes staring back at Alice's perfection. The doll remained steady before her for several seconds as she continued her descent. "Or is she the one moving?" she whispered to no one in particular.

For the first time, in what seemed like a long time, she became aware of her body. She felt hot, but the heat was emanating from within her, as if her body had gained an electric charge. The space between her eyebrows ached, but the pain was a relief to her, like stretching after waking up from a deep sleep at the end of a long train ride and having no idea where in the world you might be. The danger of not knowing where she was took her hostage.

"Where am I?" she asked aloud, comfortable doing so, knowing that no one was there to listen.

Her words dissipated into a familiar silence.

"Why me?" she said. With eyes cast down, she saw a black-and-white checkered floor in the distance below her, upon which she could just barely make out her own faint shadow.

She inhaled sharply as she reached the bottom, feet first. She bent down to touch the floor, and the white-and-black marble felt like ice on her fingertips. The long, rectangular panels of the black-and-white marble made the floor look like a giant honeycomb. Rectangular spires that mirrored the disjointed rectangular pattern of the floor constructed the white domed ceiling, making the entire place look like a large beehive that extended infinitely upward. One long corridor stretched out before her, and seemed to bend around a corner far ahead.

"I must have fallen asleep," she said, as she began rubbing her eyes. "This is, by far, the strangest meditation I have ever had in my life." She tugged at the fragile skin until her eyes watered. The red tracks that formed on her arms and shoulder blades as she raked her nails across them immediately faded away. "Why can't I wake up?" she asked frantically, as she squinted her eyes shut, bracing herself for a slap. The smacking sound echoed off the walls of the corridor in front of her. "Fine," she said, blinking her watery eyes open. "If I'm not asleep, I must have lost my way."

Or have I lost myself?

Just then, a rustling sound coming from the end of the corridor abruptly interrupted her thoughts. As she turned toward the noise, she caught a glimpse of a shadow bending itself around the wall, shying away from the faint glow projected from the rabbit hole.

"Hello?" Elizabeth pleaded, hoping for someone to answer but not to come too close. She heard more scuffling, followed by a hurried slide across the marble floor.

Elizabeth ran toward the sound. Though she had no idea how far these halls stretched, she picked up speed as she inched closer to the impetuous presence. For as fast as she ran, neither her lungs nor her leg muscles began to burn.

The coming and going of sensations added to her disori-
entation, and the chronic ache between her eyebrows grew
stronger by the minute. As she became aware of her own
footfalls, she heard the other's footsteps grow louder, and
she nearly tripped as the realization struck her that the footsteps she followed sounded much like her own.

Each step brought her closer to the footfalls that mimicked
her own, until she reached one particularly short hallway.

Just before the figure was able to completely round the
corner, Elizabeth caught a glimpse of a blue dress trailing
behind a figure with blonde hair. For a moment, the sky blue
fabric seemed to catch on a rogue splinter hiding on the wall,
as Alice tried to round the corner. Elizabeth watched the fabric rip ever so slightly as Alice freed herself, and her footsteps
once again echoed in the hallway of the marble labyrinth that
surrounded them.

Elizabeth stood fixed on the white marble tile with one
arm stretched out toward Alice, but Alice would not turn to
face her.

"Alice!" she shouted. Her voice pierced through the sound
of scuffling, as she broke into a run again. She called after
her again, her voice shrill to the point of cracking, as she lost
herself deeper within the labyrinth. "Please wait, Alice!" she
begged, her voice labored.

Alice's pace did not slow, and neither did Elizabeth's.

"I'm lost! Alice, I'm lost! I need your help!" she shouted,
nearly losing her footing as she slid across the smooth surface
of the tile.

With the bang of a door, the sound of quickened footfalls
in the distance stopped.

Alice disappeared, leaving Elizabeth at the end of a hallway. She found herself facing another corridor, with nothing but a white side table and a large black door at the opposite end. Even though she was alone when she reached the bottom of the rabbit hole, the loneliness she felt now took another, more sinister form. It was as if she could only hear one note of her favorite song, or as if she was lost in the desert and could see a plane flying far overhead.

Elizabeth's breaths became shallow as isolation gripped her. She stood frozen in the spot where she had watched Alice disappear.

"Alice!" she screamed. "Alice, can you hear me? Please stop, Alice! I know it's you, I know who you are!"

She heard only the echo of her own voice, repeating her words back to her in a fading chorus, *Alice! Alice! Alice! Know who you are! Who you are!*

How could she just disappear?

Everything she knew of reality and logic slowly slipped through her fingers, like sand in an hourglass. She reached down to touch the small nail that jutted ever so slightly out of the wall, on which Alice's dress had snagged. Several fibers of the blue dress were still caught on the nail, and Elizabeth ran her fingers over the light blue threads, as if they were something both precious and familiar.

Regaining her senses, the desperation of being alone gripped her throat once again. She raced toward the door. When she stood before it, she cautiously reached for the doorknob, but her outstretched fingers slid right through it. She saw her fingertips faintly on the other side of the door, as if she had reached her hand through a cloud. Her heart sank into her stomach, and the thought of losing Alice held her mind captive.

How could I have lost her? Oh, God. Please don't leave me alone!

"Breathe, just breathe," she reminded herself. "If Alice got through this door, then there must be a way out for me."

Scanning her surroundings for another way out and refusing to succumb to the dark fear welling up inside of her, her eyes suddenly found the small, white table that sat just a few feet to her right, which she had passed on the way to the door.

She approached the table. There was nothing on its surface, but inside of the top drawer, Elizabeth found a small, white compact with pink borders stamped across its sides. She picked it up and stashed it in her back pocket, carefully and without opening it. Beneath it she found a letter with the words *OPEN ME* handwritten on the front. The letters came together in a unique cursive that bent together like tree branches, beckoning her into their welcoming arms.

As she held the letter in her wet palms she could feel the beating of her heart inside her chest. It hummed along with the sound of a distant clock, both emitting a beat like a war drum—a harsh reminder of her seclusion and that Alice was getting farther and farther away. She tore at the letter's seams and extracted the folded paper inside, which read:

So, you want to see my world?

Look around you. Honestly, did you really think that you were going to come and do a little sightseeing? There are no maps down here, but I'll tell you what one would look like if such a thing existed. What you see around you is the white, tender underbelly of the subconscious. This is where all of the skeletons, ghosts, and demons hidden in your closet and up your sleeve come to tuck themselves in at night. And don't think for a second that they'll be easy to spot, because everyone wears a mask here. And you do, too, gorgeous, even if you don't think so. I'm not the one who looks in the mirror and then quickly looks away.

No, this isn't rock bottom. I've been to rock bottom, and I'll tell you something about it that no one ever talks about—down there it's finally quiet.

So I'll let you in on a little secret before you find yourself hopelessly lost in the depths of your own subconscious that you've fallen into. There aren't any cute little white rabbits for you to follow around, and there are no refreshments or frosted cookies that turn you into something else, or someone you're not.

When you were casually meandering down the rabbit hole, I was the one who screamed at you to run, but you didn't listen to me. That's about to change. There's something that you need to know about this place before you start following your intuitive whims instead of following my advice: You created this place. You created everything in it, and you have the free will to change and create anything you please, if you can figure out how. And when you were thinking earlier, "Oh, God. Why me?" I would like to remind you that you wanted to come here. You came here yourself. You let yourself in.

And yes, the rumors are true. Everyone here is mad. Therefore, I'm mad, too.

Welcome to Wonderland—catch me if you can, bitch.

—Alice

Three

Elizabeth's hands shook as she took in each stroke of Alice's curly script etched in black ink.

"Forget it!" Elizabeth shouted. "I don't need to prove myself to anyone! And definitely not to some doll I had when I was a kid. This isn't a meditation. This is a nightmare!" she sighed. "I'm going back."

With a huff, Elizabeth let the letter fall to the floor and spun around only to feel her nose hit a slab of cold marble. A wall had formed behind her where the hallway once was.

She let out a moan and rubbed her nose, realizing that it didn't hurt at all. "Nice one!" she said, as she bent down to retrieve the letter. "That's sarcasm, Alice, in case you can hear me."

I know there's more to this, she thought, as her mind began to run away with her, just as fast as Alice had moments ago.

For the first time in a meditation, Elizabeth wondered if she had gone too far. This is what she wanted out of a meditation, after all, to shine a light in each dark corner of herself, even if she wasn't ready for it. She considered that when it's time to come face to face with our true selves, we're never really ready. She sighed as she thought back on her morning and felt the absence of the pills that coursed through her system before plunging into this world. She admitted to herself that this felt more real than any meditation she had ever had before.

After a few more minutes of falling prey to her thoughts, Elizabeth felt a tap on her shoulder. It was Doubt and Worry.

They were brothers, twins, although they looked nothing alike. Doubt, wrapped in cashmere and wearing glasses with no lenses, is the big brother who douses self-worth with gasoline and then drops a match. Worry is the ashes, the smoke that rises and only clears with a thick breeze of clarity. The brothers crept into her mind, and yet she found herself unable to turn back. The space around her became engulfed in a mysterious murkiness, as if a quiet curtain of darkness had fallen around her without her noticing.

She bit the inside of her cheek so hard she tasted blood. "My meditation led me this far," she whispered under her breath. "Let's see what monsters live down here." She knew that if she couldn't escape Wonderland, they couldn't either.

There was only one direction for her to go: forward. She folded the letter and slid it into her left-hand back pocket, not wanting it to mingle with the mirror in the pocket on the right, and stared at the door before her. A faint light peered through the cracks on all sides, illuminating its outline in a way that made it look like a ghost.

How do I get this thing open? Elizabeth wondered, as she stood before the door she watched Alice disappear through. She reached out to touch it again, and once more, her hand slipped through, appearing on the other side. Alice's words were still murmuring in the background of her thoughts.

After a few futile tries, she looked up at the ceiling in frustration.

"If I created a door, I would want to know where it led," Elizabeth said. "I have to create the place behind the door first! It has to be the place that Alice was running to. Where was she going? Or, if I were Alice, where would I go?"

As she asked the last question, she shut her eyes and envisioned what the place behind the door might look like. An image flashed before her mind's eye, and then came to rest in the ache between her brows. The image of a meadow, lined with a hedgerow of rose bushes that encircled a grassy courtyard, took form. In the middle of the meadow courtyard stood a large tree, like the grand old oak trees in Central Park that she passed by on her way to work.

She imagined herself wading through the shade of those trees in the park, like being wrapped in a warm embrace, as if she were a part of the tree itself. She was the smallest leaf to the thickest limb. She was the bird gently nesting in the branches, playing hide-and-seek with the sunlight. The resonating sense of comfort that the image evoked engulfed her, and she tried to draw out the emotion to make the visualization stronger. She let the feeling of being in this place take over her senses, feeling the emotion fully as if the span of her entire life were condensed into that moment.

She pictured Adam there with her, underneath the tree. A smile bloomed across her lips as she thought about their first date after moving to New York. Elizabeth had packed a picnic basket, and Adam had carried it until they found the best spot. Everywhere there were adults chasing little kids, who were chasing squirrels and pigeons, in an endless game of inner-city tag. Elizabeth had told Adam that she thought there were more animals in the park than people, which somehow made it feel more human.

But in place of the New Yorkers, wandering toddlers, and tourists, she pictured Alice.

Doubt and Worry interrupted her visualization just as it was completed. This time they took form as faceless ghosts, the silent assassins of her imagination. They barged in on her emotional effusions and the landscape that had taken form in her head. Every time she felt Doubt and Worry make themselves at home in her mind, the image of the meadow would go black for a moment, and she would have to release a deep exhale to make it reappear.

How can I get through this door and face Alice if I can't even face myself? she thought. *That pill barely even gave me a kick. Did it wear off that fast?*

For a moment, she worried if she was having a bad reaction, and if she should have tried to get a prescription after all.

It's just a recreational thing. Just like college.

Just like college, she repeated to herself.

"When I get back to the apartment, I'm flushing them," she said aloud. "I'm promising myself, here and now, that if I get back, I will.

"—when I get back," she corrected. She knew that the only way back was to go forward. When she felt the image finally solidify in her mind, when she felt like she could hold it in her hands like a fragile treasure, she opened her eyes with resolve.

"Alice, I'm coming."

With the vision still alive and as vibrant as the marble hive around her, she reached for the doorknob. This time it was solid. Not letting the surprise of her own victory take her out of the moment, she took a deep inhale and pushed through the door. The light was so bright that Elizabeth's temples stung, as she walked cautiously through the door. She shut the door, and it disappeared behind her, fading to black like the marble labyrinth, sealing her inside the sepulchre of her subconscious playground.

As her eyes adjusted, she watched her new surroundings come to life around her. The sky looked like glass. It was a washed-out gray-blue, as if a storm had just passed. Her eyes moved over the scene before her, which included a meadow lined with hedgerows of rose bushes.

To the last red petal, it was exactly the way she envisioned it to be.

Elizabeth looked over to an old oak tree in the center of the meadow courtyard. It was bent and cracked with age. She stared at it with curiosity and realized that it floated in the air, its roots exposed. Because the tree had no leaves, and because the roots and the branches were both so broad, she couldn't decide which were which, or if, in fact, the tree was dangling upside down. It seemed to mirror itself, as it hung over the long flowing grass of the meadow.

Even though the tree looked dead, there was something

about it that seemed very alive to her. She had certainly never seen a floating tree before, let alone one that might be upside down or right side up.

Despite the novelty of the tree, Elizabeth's eyes widened as she gazed at the scene unfolding beneath it. There was a large group of animals engaged in mumbling conversation at the base of the tree, though she was unsure if they were conversing or merely speaking loudly over one another. There were several mice, a badger, a white crane, a turtle, a few ducks, a small black bear, two lizards, and a squawking parrot, all of whom were babbling unintelligibly. Just then, she noticed a black raven standing curiously silent in the shade of a tall hedgerow.

"A floating tree, a menagerie of animals, and no Alice in sight," she sighed. "I explicitly pictured Alice! Or at least Adam." She stared at the group of misfits, all mumbling at once, loitering beneath the ungrounded oak tree without distinct direction or intention.

"Well, at least they look friendly," Elizabeth grumbled. "Maybe they could tell me where Alice is. Or where I am, exactly."

As she approached the group, she was aware of each footstep. She felt the grass bow beneath her feet and continued to stay connected to her breath. To her surprise, none of the animals seemed to notice her at all. With each footfall, she expected at least one of the animals to stop their conversation and turn toward her, but as she drew nearer to the group, not one of them looked up.

"It's so loud," she murmured to herself. "Like the hallways at my old high school!" When she entered the meadow courtyard, their mumbling became louder, though it was still indistinguishable. She realized they were each talking to themselves.

Still, no one noticed her.

The badger happened to be closest to her, as she joined the band of creatures in the meadow courtyard, in the broken shade of the hovering tree. Though she was standing beside him, enveloping him in darkness as she cast her shadow over him, he did not turn around. The badger took occasional staccato steps in between long pauses, while managing to keep up his conversation with himself all the same.

"I don't know. I suppose I could take a vacation. But where would I go?" the badger contemplated aloud to himself. "I should probably finish work on the burrow first. I never finish anything I start, it seems."

"Excuse me?" Elizabeth said.

"Ava is always saying that to me, that I need to be more persistent," the badger continued. "That's just the thing with me, no follow-through. Ava said it herself. Although I can follow a nice dance step!"

"I don't want to interrupt you, but can I ask you what's going on?" Elizabeth said in a louder tone.

"I haven't danced in so long! I really need to take Ava out sometime," the badger reflected. "She always says I'm such a homebody. Am I a homebody?"

It seemed that he asked the question only to himself, as he never made eye contact with Elizabeth despite the fact that the pitch of her voice rose steadily, almost to a yell.

"Just a second," Elizabeth reached out and tapped the badger on the shoulder. He didn't notice.

"Home!" he exclaimed. "Speaking of home, I need to do a little spring cleaning! Then maybe Ava will stop nagging me about it."

Doubt and Worry whispered in her ear.

Why can't he hear me? Maybe I didn't believe my own visualization hard enough, maybe that's why it didn't come out the way I wanted it to. Or, maybe I should have pictured a badger with a little more focus.

Her shoulders slouched, and she continued on. From what she had seen of badgers along the road in the real world, they did always seem to be lost.

The small black bear paced on two legs a few feet away from her. As Elizabeth approached him, he seemed lost in his own world. She stood right next to him, but he didn't look up.

"Talk to me," Elizabeth said, more forcefully than with the badger. Her introduction was met with no reply.

"Those berries I found yesterday were simply intoxicating," the bear considered. "Where did I find those?"

"Ahem," Elizabeth coughed, as she tried to lean down and catch his line of sight.

"I know I've seen those berries somewhere around here before," the bear said, as a quizzical look spread across his face. One paw rested on his hip and the other paw, with one long claw jutting out, tapped his nose, as he puzzled over his thoughts. For a moment, their eyes met, but it was as if he looked right through her.

"This is hopeless!" Elizabeth sighed.

Doubt and Worry placed their hands on her shoulder in comfort. *Am I not guilty of following the whims of my own thoughts?* She thought back to her morning with Adam and all the other mornings she had spent staring through Adam, as he had tried to tell her something. Looking through him instead of at him. She swore to herself that it wasn't for lack of caring that kept her from getting lost in her own world, from becoming like the animals around her.

She looked up at the tree and tried to ground herself in the same sense of calm that she felt when she first imagined its existence. She thought again of the trees she sat under with Adam. She remembered looking up into the web of branches like it was a labyrinth, and she'd lean back on her hands, which would bump into Adam's hands. He would inevitably lace his fingers around hers, like the crossed branches above them. She nibbled at the inside of her cheek at the thought; the wound from the hallway earlier seemed to have disappeared.

Elizabeth then approached the group of mice who stirred in the middle of the crowd a few feet to her left.

"Excuse me, everyone, please," Elizabeth pleaded in vain. She discovered that the mice weren't even speaking to one another, despite the fact that they stood in a circle facing each another. They each seemed to be unaware of the other mice, let alone her presence.

"I don't know why Henry assumes I like cheese. Is it because I'm a mouse? That's so cliché. What is he trying to say? That I'm simple and predictable? It's like he thinks I'm boring! What a joke," the first mouse grumbled, his whiskers shaking with anger.

"I feel like there must be something I should be doing right now. All of this standing around is making me antsy. Maybe I should start looking for dinner," a second mouse contemplated aloud.

"And so I said to myself, Henry, you're just going to have to find another group of friends, some mice who understand you," Henry bemoaned. "And then he goes and proves me right by stealing my cheese right in front of me . . . and then denies it! He said he doesn't even like cheese in the first place! Does he think I'm stupid?"

"Henry, please," Elizabeth said, crouching down to her knees in front of the mouse so he could hear her. "Your name is Henry, right? I don't want to interrupt, but no one here is paying attention to anything. No one even pays attention to the world around them long enough to let me interrupt them!"

"He just doesn't get it. He doesn't understand me at all," Henry carried on.

Elizabeth gave up on Henry and turned to a third mouse, who was light brown with a long pink tail. He spoke so quickly she could hardly make out what he was saying.

"First, I need to make sure I find a drier place to live in, then I'll be happy," the mouse said quickly. "A place of my very own without other mice to get in my way and tell me what to do. If I could just be by myself, without so many other mice, I think then I would be happy. After that, I think I should find myself a more suitable job, something that makes me feel like a real mouse. Once I find that, then I'll be happy. I'll be able to hoard all of the scraps I can find and keep them all to myself, because I'll live in a place where I won't have to be burdened by other mice. That's true happiness! I'll never be unhappy after I achieve all of that."

Elizabeth then turned to the mouse directly next to him who had long white hair and who wore a pair of small dark sunglasses, despite the lack of sun.

"Can you hear me? Are you stuck in this nightmare, too?" Elizabeth said with sadness in her voice.

"Surely the right mouse for me is out there somewhere. Someone who likes the things I like, who's a little bit bigger than me, with a long tail. There's nothing like feeling a long tail wrapped around mine, cuddling next to a warm fire! There must be someone who enjoys that too, and who'll think I'm interesting and listen to my stories. He could even be right in front of me, and I might not even know it! Oh, the thought of it," the blind mouse daydreamed aloud.

Elizabeth looked at the two remaining mice, both the same shade of gray, who stood next to one another in the circle and yet complained of being dreadfully alone.

"These mice aren't any better than the bear or the badger," she said, as she felt her stomach sink. "And then there's me. Standing in this meadow, talking to myself."

She looked back to the tree floating a few feet off the ground, its roots tickling the grass below. She thought to herself, *I'm no better than they are, because I'm lost, too. In a way, we are each our own animal, deluded by the illusion that we're all separate from one another.*

As she suddenly became aware of her thoughts, the illusion of separateness began to fade away, like the door she had walked through into Wonderland. She looked around her. Across from her, the ducks trotted, each following the others' tail and quacking complaints that were completely unrelated to their siblings. There was a small dandelion near them, its bright yellow petals standing in stark contrast to the pale green of the meadow grass around it, which the ducks trampled over without notice. To the side of the ducks, stood the white crane, who remained still but could be heard ferociously humming a line of a song over and over again that Elizabeth could not quite make out.

Maybe Bach?

She stood next to the tree, looking out over the crowd of chattering animals. The squawking parrot was the loudest. He circled a few feet away from her next to the ducks. He repeated fragments of conversations that didn't seem to be his own, as she heard him remark that he was a lucky beaver for having found such a big log.

"I've seen bigger logs than that. I mean, that log was fine, if you're into small logs," the parrot cawed, inserting his own opinion. "Brandon's log was bigger and looked much more sturdy. Beatrice said she would never move in with him with a log that size, and she accepted an invitation from Brandon to come visit his!"

"How can he stand here and repeat gossip all day? Doesn't he run out of rumors after awhile?" she mused. "What does he have to do with beavers? Unless birds here can turn themselves into beavers, and so far I'm not sure if that would surprise me."

The incessant squawking began to make her temples hurt again, with pain also throbbing in the space between her eyebrows. She turned away from the parrot and saw two lizards facing off behind her. She had hardly noticed them over the parrot's ranting. The hair on the back of her neck stood on end, as she overheard them verbally plotting the other's demise, though they were looking each other directly in the eye.

"He'll never see it coming," the first lizard said, with his long, blue tail curling in delight.

"He's probably watching me," the second lizard said in a deep voice, with his red body aflame with paranoid shudders. "I'll have no choice but to attack him from behind. He'll never see it coming."

"I'll take him by surprise from the back! It's a perfect plan," the blue lizard said, as his forked tongue tasted the air.

Shivers ran down her arms like tiny ants, and she resolved to move away from them before their thoughts escalated. As she stepped away from them, she nearly stepped on the turtle, whose slow pace seemed to contradict the speed of his thoughts. His words came out so fast they were strung along out of sequence. He skipped over some words entirely, as a rock skips over water.

"I just . . . never again have I seen . . . the chrysalis was so high . . . looked something like a star, it was so high up there . . . wiggling in the wind."

He seemed to be reliving a moment in such vivid detail that he didn't notice he was caught in a large clump of meadow grass, and so he tried to move forward to no avail, like a wind-up toy caught on a rug.

Elizabeth stopped again, finding herself in the same spot she had started from, next to the badger, who was still talking about Ava. She wandered through the meadow courtyard, only to find that each animal wasn't really in the meadow courtyard at all. It was no wonder they couldn't see her, because they couldn't see themselves. They might be walking, but they didn't feel the ground beneath their feet, paws, or talons. They were numb to the present moment, escaping into the retreats of their minds. They complained about being alone, and yet there was a meadow courtyard full of animals who were doing the same things and feeling the same way.

Suddenly, Elizabeth laughed. She wondered how we could ever feel lonely when we're all just like the animals, walking in circles around a tree in a meadow courtyard, feeling alone while being surrounded by others just like us. To her, that was true insanity.

A light breeze moved through her long, black hair, though she didn't feel it on her skin. She felt each strand of hair dancing. Then she felt the folded, crushed grass beneath her boots. She felt the uneven ground and shifted her balance. She felt the air in her lungs. If there were a sun or a moon, she would have felt its energy, as well. But rather, she felt the energy of the tree before her, with its roots and branches exposed, and she felt a deep sadness that its beauty was lost to the creatures around it. She felt life, and all of the mad and beautiful energy that made its flesh and bones.

"I have to make them notice me!" she said. She wanted to

free them from their mental prisons, so they could see they weren't alone. She wondered how she could make them see themselves when she could barely do it herself.

Elizabeth's gaze darted around her, and she took in each little detail of her surroundings like never before. Immediately, her gaze fell upon the one creature whose presence she had almost overlooked. The black raven stood silently at the edge of the meadow courtyard, hidden in the shadows of the hedgerow.

She marched directly toward him, stepping over the turtle, muttering her pardons to the badger, the mice, the ducks, the crane, and the bear, all of whom maintained their own musings without noticing her. Finally, she got on her hands and knees to look the raven in his deep black eyes. He remained silent, staring at her with eyes that appeared glazed over.

"I know you see me!" Elizabeth shouted. "Please!"

His beak chattered with words unspoken. He was far away. She knew she needed him to look at her, to really see her. After snapping, clapping, uttering absurd birdcalls, stroking the bird's feathers, and hitting her fists against the grassy floor, he remained unmoved. Elizabeth stopped for a moment to catch her breath.

"I need help. I need a sign," Elizabeth sighed, her eyes still closed.

Suddenly, she felt the weight of her back pocket, and she reached for her compact.

"Maybe I don't need him to see me," she smiled. "I just need him to see himself."

But there was no sunlight for Elizabeth to catch with the

mirror, to signal the raven as you would signal a ship lost in the night.

Kneeling on her hands and knees before him she opened the compact and, without looking into it, she held it up in between her eyebrows to face him. The raven's eyes were reflected back to him. Elizabeth had never seen a bird blink before. She wasn't sure if they could, but the raven's energy began to change, as if he had woken up from a dream. He was staring at himself curiously, poking the mirror lightly with his beak.

"Why, hello! Hello, me!" the raven cooed, breaking his silence. He was speaking to himself.

"Um, hello," Elizabeth stuttered.

"What fine black feathers I have, and so shiny!" the raven squealed, still speaking to himself, as if Elizabeth weren't behind the mirror.

"Yes, it is I," Elizabeth clucked back, mimicking the raven's own voice to keep him talking, "Raven."

"Such handsome black eyes," the raven cawed.

"Yes, yes they are," Elizabeth mused. "Can I ask myself a question, handsome raven?"

"Yes, of course, I was just asking myself one."

"Where are we exactly?"

"We're in the meadow. Just look at all the long grasses and the hedgerows! They looked so much different from above, when I flew here."

"We flew here?" she asked hurriedly, afraid he was becoming lost in his own thoughts again. "What else did we see?"

"There was a lot of grass. No trees, I'm afraid, except for

that one. I would have landed on it, but I couldn't tell if its branches were branches or roots. So I landed here. But before I stopped for a rest, I wanted to continue into the deep forest just beyond the hedgerows, to find a nice tree to nest in, or a nice mouse to eat. These talons of mine are pretty strong. I've even scooped up more than one mouse at a time!"

For a moment, Elizabeth sighed with relief and looked over her shoulder at Henry and the group of mice a few feet away. Then she began to picture the deep forest beyond them, silently comforted by the thought of trees and of a place less exposed.

That must be where Alice went, Elizabeth thought to herself, still resting the mirror against her temple. *If I were Alice, that is exactly where I would go. She probably feels at home in the darkness.*

"Raven," Elizabeth said aloud "Have we seen a girl? A girl in a blue dress, with blonde hair?"

"Of course we have, it was the girl in the blue dress," the raven squawked suddenly. Elizabeth thought she saw him shiver.

"Are we feeling okay?"

He was silent for a moment. "She ran off into the woods, just after she passed these hedgerows, looking for a spot in the roses. She's a scary one. She took off at a sprint. I was curious to know why she ran with such confidence into woods as dark as those. If it weren't for the treetops, we wouldn't dare enter at all."

"Why's that?" Elizabeth prompted. "What's in there?"

"You mean *who's* in there. Strange creatures. A blue- and- white house, far, far away, with a garden of strange wildflowers, wildflowers like we've never seen before. We've only seen it once, and it had an odd feeling about it. It's very dark where it is, no mice, no mice at all," the raven cawed quickly. "Some twins, something floating, and horrible, noisy beings."

"Wait a second," Elizabeth proceeded carefully. "The girl in the blue dress, what was she looking for?"

"She wasn't looking. She was hiding something. Everyone hides here," the raven mused. "Actually, just the other day we hid . . ."

His eyes glassed over again.

"No, raven! Listen!" Elizabeth cawed quickly, but she lost him. His beak chattered, moving to make inaudible words again.

"Really?" she moaned. *Even Fitz has a longer attention span than that!* Elizabeth slipped the compact back into her pocket. *If I were Alice, what would I hide?* She shivered. *Actually, maybe I don't want to know. But if I had something to hide, where would I hide it?*

With Adam she hid things in plain sight, right where he would see them but never look, somewhere so obvious that he never thought twice about it. She tried to hide his old sneakers a few times. First, she put them on top of the shelf near the desk, then next to the picture frames. Another time, she hid them on top of a stack of paper near the door, where they sat for almost a week.

"Now, if I had to hide them here," she wondered aloud, "I would hide them there, at the bottom of the hedgerow, with the edges just poking out into the grass." Her eyes darted from place to place around the base of the hedgerows. "It's perfect! It's right in the open, but where only a skilled eye would know to look." She looked for a place that would attract just the person it was intended for, someone who is attuned to details and knows how to find something so obviously tucked away.

In this case, she thought, *I guess that someone is me.*

She scanned the long grasses beneath a hedgerow just behind the raven. Suddenly, she noticed a tiny, folded piece of paper next to a rose that stuck out of the hedge and the tall grass. The ink bled through the paper in some places, as if it had been written quickly, but thoughtful pauses had been made in some places. Reaching carefully around the raven, she grasped the letter and rose to her feet.

In scrawling letters, the front read *OPEN ME.*

She took a breath and tore the letter open.

Looks like you're smarter than I thought. Unfortunately, that doesn't really matter here in Wonderland. Logic and Reason aren't creatures you'll find down here.

But I can't give you all the credit—so you used the compact I left for you, what genius! There's something you should know about Wonderland, sweetie, and that's that genius is insanity, and insanity is genius. Why, of all things, do you think I chose to leave you that mirror in the first place? Obviously, not for your own use. All you would find in your reflection is a scared little girl.

Are you comfortable here, in my home? Don't hold your breath. There are woods that lie beyond this meadow courtyard, and in them you'll see things you've never seen before. Well, actually, you have—you created them yourself. But remember what I said, every-one wears masks here. Unmask them for who they are, and you might find some friends that seem more familiar than what you're comfortable with.

There I go, mentioning comfort again. This is your home, too, you know. You gave life to every blade of grass. You are every blade, and every blade is you. Even that ugly tree over there.

And if you're wondering whether the tree is, in fact, upside down, and if its branches are its roots or if its roots are its branches, the answer is that it, like me, and all you see around you, is also mad.

As usual, I'm two steps ahead of you, so hurry up.

I'm waiting.

—Alice

Four

"She's psychotic," Elizabeth fumed. "She calls me scared, but she's the one running from me!"

She squeezed the letter in her clenched fist, feeling the paper crunch between her fingers. Gone was the girl from the marble labyrinth and from the rabbit hole from which she fell. An invisible chrysalis began to crystallize around her, allowing her to transform with each passing moment.

All of the past is dead to me. The girl that I was when I reached the bottom of the rabbit hole is dead, she thought to herself. *The meditating girl is dead.*

Here and now, she died to herself each moment, being reborn with each new breath that aroused a sharp spirit within—a spirit whose hunger for answers left a maddening ache in her stomach.

"Thanks, raven," she cawed to him, though he was still trapped within the confines of his mind. She stepped over him and whizzed passed the badger, who still muttered to himself about Ava, and found her way back to the opening of the hedgerows. She gazed at the meadow around her, taking in the full sepulchre in which she had begun, one that was ornate on the outside but dead on the inside. Once more into the unknown.

As she charged through the long grass, the floating tree grew smaller and smaller behind her, until the meadow court-yard faded away, one world giving birth to the one she was about to enter.

She recalled the images that the raven described from watching Alice enter the woods. The darkness and the tall trees splattered across her mind like the Jackson Pollock that hung in the lobby of the studio she worked in.

This time I've got to get it right!

She closed her eyes and continued her pace, imagining what it would feel like to be in those woods, just as she had imagined what the meadow would feel like. A feeling of sol-itude crept in, and with it came the comfort of being hidden, like a small child playing hide-and-seek, only she was both the seeker and the one who was hidden.

The prospect of the shadows, wild branches, and leaves felt like refuge, like an advantage over Alice.

"We'll see who's two steps ahead of who!"

She continued her march through the grassy landscape of her subconscious that stretched infinitely before her. The woods slowly took form in the distance, exactly as she had pictured them in her mind, down to the last branch on the tallest tree. The start of the forest looked like a giant wall, tall and dark, guarding the secrets that lie within—the ones hiding behind thick tree trunks and nestled in tall branches.

Then, suddenly, a deranged laughter, coming from nowhere in particular, broke her concentration.

She froze.

Looking around her, she saw nothing but the meadow's long grasses and open space on all sides of her, the dark trees loomed in a haze.

"Hello?" she shouted into the wall of branches. "Alice?"

Nothing.

Where did that laughter come from? From my head? No more disembodied voices, please. The specter of Alice's voice in the rabbit hole floated across her mind, telling her to run.

"Alice? You there?" Her temples and the place between her eyes began to ache again. "Come out, unless you're scared!" Elizabeth called, her hands curled into fists.

More laughter—an unhinged sort of laughter, with erratic pauses followed by louder cackles, which turned into soft giggles and quiet snickers, and then back into rolling, guttural bellows.

"I know you're there!" Elizabeth yelled, her hand rested on her back pocket where the compact was concealed. She was ready to pull it out at a moment's notice. "Show yourself!"

"Well," the voice cackled, "all you had to do was ask!"

She looked above her to see a furry, red-orange cat. It had light orange stripes that ran haphazardly down its back, legs, and tail. The most intriguing feature of the cat was the pattern on his face, which started between his ears and ran down to the space between his eyes, just above his nose. It looked like the tribal pattern on her back pockets, except orange. He looked just like Lucifer.

"Lucifer?"

"Who?" the cat said in between snickers.

"Who are you?" Elizabeth asked. "Come down so I can see you better!"

"Who, me?" The cat giggled, rolling in the air with sharp laughter.

"Yes, you!"

"Why don't you come up here?"

"Ridiculous," Elizabeth mumbled under her breath.

"Of course you are," the cat said. "Why would you walk on the ground when you can float up here?"

"I can't float," Elizabeth shot back.

"Why not? You don't know how?"

He licked his paws as he floated down toward her. She watched him as he dipped down, stopping just before her face, hovering as the Alice doll had in the rabbit hole.

"You can't be Lucifer," she said. "He couldn't float."

"Well don't just stand there! Tell me a happy story, something to lighten the mood!"

"Are you the Cheshire Cat?" Elizabeth asked with pronounced curiosity, ignoring his request.

"Are you?" the Cat countered.

"No, I'm asking if you are."

"You are? I am. I'm the Cheshire Cat. Have we met?"

"I don't think so," Elizabeth said with a furrowed brow. "It's just that I thought you were someone else. You don't look like the Cheshire Cat . . . I thought he was purple?"

"How funny!" the Cat said as he broke into unhinged laughter again. "I thought you were blonde and wore a blue dress!"

"Whatever," Elizabeth replied as she rolled her eyes. "Could you tell me about this place?"

The Cat grinned so wide his neck could barely support the weight of his head, and he clapped along with the syllables as he sang: "Her mind had gone out for a stroll, and then fell down the rabbit hole!"

"Sure . . . the rabbit hole. Then that definitely means this place is—"

"Wonderland! Or I'm in Wonderland, at least."

"I don't understand where Wonderland is, exactly," Elizabeth persisted. "Is it all in my head, or did I fall asleep? I mean, this can't be a real place. Can it?"

"Wonderland is being everywhere and nowhere, all at once," the Cheshire Cat said, as he grinned a disturbing smile.

Or was it a smirk? she thought to herself, just as Doubt and Worry joined the conversation. *Can I not get an honest answer out of anybody? Is everyone here truly mad?*

"Obviously," the Cheshire Cat replied with a serious look on his face.

"You heard what I was thinking just now?"

"You think very loudly, dear. It's not polite."

"Sorry," she said. "But I was under the impression that my thoughts were private!"

"Who gave you that idea?"

"Look, it's just that I don't feel very much like myself today. I had a rough morning. I fought with Adam and started questioning myself. Ever since I fell down the rabbit hole everything stopped making sense," Elizabeth said, as she felt herself rambling, giving Doubt and Worry a new form with each word. "I need to find a girl, Alice, the one with the blue dress. I think you know her. Only I don't know my way around here, and sometimes I feel like I'm just making it up as I go—"

"How wonderful!" the Cat interjected excitedly.

"Wonderful?"

"It *is* Wonderland, after all!"

"I've had just about enough of Wonderland! If everyone here is like those animals in the meadow courtyard, then I might as well be walking with ghosts. Alice told me that this place was like the 'white underbelly' of the subconscious, but from what I've seen I think I must be clenched in its teeth instead," Elizabeth said.

"The teeth of a beast? What an interesting idea," the Cat said with wide green eyes, which flashed a look that Elizabeth could only characterize as psychotic. "I always pictured this place as more of an onion. The subconscious peels like an onion, after all. You peeled off the first layer over there. The surface was merely meaningless, futile ego babble. But the way all the layers are wound together . . . It's genius! Sheer genius!"

Suddenly, Alice's words clawed their way to the surface of her mind: *There is something you should know about Wonderland, sweetie, and that's that genius is insanity, and insanity is genius.*

"See!" the Cat purred. "You know!"

"What's next, then? What else does the ego have to offer? Silence? More solitude?"

She thought of her purple toothbrush ricocheting against the porcelain sink. She thought of her messy bathroom, and how she could never get her hair just right. She thought of the wrinkles in her work shirts that she said she would iron out but never did. She thought of the window that never shut tight enough, the pants that never fit right, and how she always lost her pen caps and chewed her nails. She thought of the hours where her mind held a gun to her head, and the thoughts, like greasy henchmen, who never left her alone.

"What do you fear, Elizabeth?"

She crossed her arms.

"Come on," he goaded with a purr.

"Being lost," she said at last. "In thoughts, or being lost to myself."

"Do you feel lost now?"

"I've been lost this whole time."

"How do you know you're lost?"

Elizabeth rolled her eyes.

"We're all lost, or we're all not lost at all," he said with a grin. "We're all just looking for ourselves in the dark woods." Then the Cheshire Cat laughed a laugh so deep that his orange body shook where he floated. He laughed so hard that he almost choked. Elizabeth took a few steps back, in case he coughed up a hairball. He hacked and wheezed until a spark left his mouth, which fizzled before her eyes, like a sparkler burning out just before it reaches your fingertips.

Elizabeth didn't know if she should rush to his side, or run.

"Excuse me!" he sputtered. "That was frightful. Silence, you say! What a laugh. 'Silence.' You don't find silence with an ego, my dear," the Cheshire Cat said, recovering from his fit. "You find silence only in the absence of your mind, where there is Nothing. Not even You."

"I see," she said, not exactly sure if she was following what he was saying, though it didn't feel like nonsense either. "I hope to find 'Nothing' in the woods over there. I'm looking for Alice."

The Cat furrowed his brows, making the orange-striped

tribal pattern between his eyes look like the twisted path of a labyrinth.

"Why are you looking for her?"

"Did you listen to anything I just said?" Elizabeth asked. "I told you just a minute ago that I need to find her, remember? Do you know her?"

"Know who? You?"

"No, know Alice!"

"I know what I know, and that's all that I know."

"Oh please," she said. "Don't act like you don't know what I'm talking about! It's like I'm speaking nonsense to you, isn't it?"

"If you were speaking nonsense, my dear, I would understand you perfectly! It's this non-nonsense that confuses me," the Cat said, and then began licking his paws again.

"If I knew how to speak any other way, I would," Elizabeth sighed. "I'm sure there must be someone here I can speak to, maybe someone in the woods—"

"The woods!" the Cat exclaimed. "It's fun in there. Many monsters."

"Monsters?"

"Yes, I defeated a few myself," said the Cat with a twisted smile, as he shifted to hover upside down. Regardless of his physical orientation, he maintained the same maniacal grin and the same demented flare in his eyes, like the eyes of a madman.

How could I have possibly thought he was Lucifer? They looked identical, except for the lack of Lucifer's red collar.

"Who?" asked the Cat.

"Forget it," she said. "Just tell me, how do I defeat the monsters? Alice said there would be friends in the woods, not monsters. But to Alice, maybe they're the same. Or is it that friends wear the masks of monsters?"

"That's why I smile!" the Cat bellowed, purring with glee.

"Oh, *that's* why?" Elizabeth asked, as sarcasm dripped from her lips. "That gets rid of the monsters, just like that?"

"That's how you defeat monsters, my dear. You let them see you smiling."

She looked deeply into his green eyes then tilted her head slightly, taking in the full caricature of him. A portion of the top of his left ear was missing. The fur around his neck was pressed down in a thin line, as if it had collapsed under the weight of a collar that had since disappeared.

"Alright, sure," muttered Elizabeth. "I guess I should go meet these monsters for myself. Please, though, will you answer my question?" she paused. "Do you really know Alice? Could you tell me how to find her?"

"You know the way!" the Cat giggled. "You paved it yourself! And if you should need me, simply think of me and ask."

Then she watched the Cheshire Cat dissolve before her eyes. His tail vanished first, followed by his paws, body, and ears. Then his eyes and whiskers faded slowly, leaving only the pattern of the orange labyrinth between his eyes along with his twisted, mad grin.

Finally, she stood alone with her thoughts again.

He really did look just like Lucifer. I must be losing it.

The forest wall grew closer with each step. The idea of monsters began to take root in her mind, and it mushroomed into a fear that accompanied the uncertainty of what she might find in the darkness, where the wild and horrible things mingled and shook hands like old friends.

Suddenly she nearly tripped over nothing, pitched forward from the force of Doubt and Worry's hands on her back. She wondered if by entering the woods she could be falling into Alice's trap. She went over Alice's letters in her mind and decided that Alice didn't want her in Wonderland. She regained her balance and stood there, questioning whether she wanted to peel away Wonderland's next layer, like the Cheshire Cat had said.

Suddenly, the gap closed between her and the skinny, twisted trees that lined the forest's edge. Without warning, she found herself at the threshold of darkness, face to face with a wall of towering trees.

Wedged in the middle of the trees between two pillars of black-and-white stones stood something more sinister, something she hadn't seen from where she had conversed with the Cheshire Cat. A rusted wrought-iron gate stood ajar before her, as if someone had opened it in a hurry and had forgotten to latch it behind them.

An iron signpost attached at the top of the two pillars glared back at her with ten metal letters that melded together to form cursive script. The twisted metal read: *WONDERLAND.*

Five

Elizabeth entered and the rusty gate closed with a cry behind her.

She stood still for a moment and eyed the bright green moss crawling up the black trees that spiraled endlessly above her. In some areas, the forest seemed to be almost devoid of color. The trees were black, and the open space that separated them consisted of hazy shades of blue and gray. The tall trees and their bony branches cast long shadows that fell upon Elizabeth in streaks, reminding her of prison bars. In some places, where the trees were less dense, the light broke through, setting Wonderland on fire with its brightness. The crushed leaves that lay on the forest floor emitted brilliant hues of red, brown, yellow, and orange, like an old Persian carpet, and the air around her had a misty blue hue. Elizabeth's eyes lingered on the trees the most, though. They were black oak trees with aged, cracked wood, sporting branches bereft of leaves that jutted outward at sharp angles away from the trunk and pointed straight upward.

They look like living, breathing forks! she thought, though she wondered if it was really the other way around.

She crept carefully through the trail of leaves. The areas of the forest that seemed gray entwined with the more colorful areas without rhyme or reason. Because there was no sun, the light streaked through the trees haphazardly, creating dark shadows against bright, side by side with streaks of light. With no doors in sight, she felt alone again.

"I guess if I don't know exactly where I'm going, it doesn't matter which way I go," she said as she threw her hands up in frustration. "If I were Alice, which way would I go?"

Every path looked the same. The prong-like tree branches twisted and tangled as their crooked tips crossed high overhead, ensnaring her in a labyrinth of bark, wood, and rotted leaves. So she chose a path with color and light. Because she had no other means of navigation, she knew she only had her heart to follow.

Though branches and leaves cracked in a symphony underneath her boots, her breath was the only sound she listened to. Occasionally she would hear a strange noise—a caw or a chirp from some shadowy place in the forked branches above her, or a rustling sound coming from other places out of sight, as if something was trying to remain hidden. Like the forest itself was hiding.

Then there were instances when Elizabeth thought she heard the sound of faint laughter.

"Someone there?" Elizabeth shouted to the trees around her. "Hello?"

More silence.

"It doesn't sound like the Cheshire Cat," she sighed. *I must be losing my mind. Where are all the monsters Alice warned me about?*

I haven't seen anyone for miles, she thought to herself. "Maybe she was just trying to scare me, to get me to stop following her. Nice try, Alice, but I'm still—"

Her sentence was interrupted by the sound of disjointed, rapturous laughs, this time louder and coming from one of the trees nearby. Then, as quickly as she heard it, it quieted.

Alice's voice echoed through her mind, telling her to turn around before it was too late. *Maybe I should run,* she thought, as she stopped for a moment to rest against the thick trunk of one of the forked oaks. *Run as fast as I can until I can't run anymore, until I fall asleep and wake up back in my apartment with Adam and Fitz.*

"Alice wouldn't have come this far," Elizabeth thought aloud this time, as she looked up at the gray sky. "And how long has she been in here? Time's just another form of nonsense here."

"Hoo, hoo, who are you?" shouted a scared voice from overhead.

She looked up and saw a bird nesting in the branch above her. The bird jostled around in its nest, careful not to break the eggs beneath her. The bird was blue, with an elegant chest that boasted puffy white feathers. She was a small bird, but her voice was not a reflection of her size.

"Sorry, I thought I was alone! Didn't mean to frighten you," Elizabeth called to her. "Actually, I'm glad you called! I'm lost."

"You think you can trick me, serpent? You're not welcome here!" the bird hissed with fear in her eyes. She danced uneasily around her nest, growing more anxious by the second.

"Serpent? No, I'm a girl! Can't you see me?"

"Of course I can! You're a snake! Think I haven't seen a snake before?"

"I'm sure you've seen a snake before, but I promise you that I'm not one. See? Two legs!" Elizabeth shouted, as she stuck one leg after the other out in front of her. Her leather leggings glinted in the light like black scales.

"Legs, she says! Funny! And anyway, what's the difference? Stay away from my eggs!" the bird sang fiercely. "Get back! You're not welcome here! These snakes always think they can trick me into leaving my nest, they think they can scare me. Not today!"

Elizabeth looked up at the sky. "This is ridiculous. Why do you think I'm a snake? My name is Elizabeth, I'm a girl. I walk on two legs. It's not like I have a forked tongue," she said. She stuck her tongue out at the bird, the way she would have when she was five.

"On the outside, sure! No one is who, or what, they appear to be. I know there's an ugly snake somewhere inside of you!"

"On the inside of me you would find organs. I'm flesh and blood, nothing more," she said, as she threw her arms up. "If you could just tell me where to go, I'll leave!"

"Of course there's no snake inside your physical body, that's nonsense! I mean deeper within, so deep that it's too dark to see it. You don't even know it's there. I know there's a serpent in there, I can smell it!"

Elizabeth fell silent for a moment, as the bird shuffled uneasily in her small nest, loosening a few small twigs, which fell on Elizabeth like snowflakes. "As far as I know, there's no snake within me. Maybe I don't know all of what's below the surface, but who does?"

"You may not have met the serpent yet," the bird chirped back with a ferocity that made Elizabeth take a step back. "Now get away from my nest. This is the last time I'll ask nicely!"

With this, the bird began to cry a warning chirp so loud that Elizabeth covered her ears. She kept them covered as she silently retreated. Even after the tree and the nest were out of sight, she could still hear the bird faintly from afar, like a lonely car alarm echoing a few blocks away on a quiet night.

Left with her thoughts, Elizabeth kicked at the leaves as she walked, wondering if the bird had seen something in her that she didn't know was there, and if it was possible that something could hide so deep within you that you cease to know it. She parted the branches around her, looking for a new path to follow. There was something about this place that made everything seem both possible and impossible all at once. There were paradoxes and absurdities around every corner, coexisting under a moonless sky. As she continued her walk through the dark forest of Wonderland, the paradoxes began to seem more real than the reality to which she so desperately clung.

After some time passed, she began to remember her breath, which was labored but present. Sure as the feeling of the tide coming in. As she reconnected to this lifeline, she took her time and paid attention to the details of the forest around her, as she wound herself around the paths between the trees.

"I need a sign. Anything! I can't spend the rest of my life

wandering," she said. She reminded herself that she found Alice's letter by staying grounded and present and allowing herself to recognize the little signs around her. She felt the weight of the letter in her back pocket. When living outside of the present moment, there are certain gifts that go unnoticed, and it was no different in Wonderland, where galaxies could perhaps be hidden under a rock, waiting to be found.

Elizabeth stumbled upon one such gift that took the form of an oddly placed shadow in the middle of a small clearing.

She stood in front of a clearing of tall grass where no trees seemed to grow. Yet, despite the lack of trees, there was a crescent-shaped shadow in the middle of the clearing. Its presence didn't make sense to her at all. Slowly she walked over to the shadow until she stood on top of it and looked up. Up there, woven between the tall, forked branches that surrounded the edge of the clearing, hung a chrysalis.

How did this get here?

A large chrysalis, half her size, hung above the darkness of the woods as if it had always been there, and would always be there.

As she circled beneath it, staring up at it with wide eyes, Elizabeth writhed within her own chrysalis, experiencing a metamorphosis taking place deep within her, though what she might be changing into eluded her.

Just then, the chrysalis began to stir.

"Oh no," Elizabeth gulped. After her experience with the bird, she began to think that she was better off alone after all. The chrysalis danced, swinging like a ballet dancer suspended in the air. Mesmerized, Elizabeth stood transfixed beneath it.

Alice? she wondered.

As she stood there, the chrysalis began to tear from the inside out. She clenched her jaw and took a few steps back.

The chrysalis, which once had been dull in color, seemed to transform into something black mixed with a deep red, the color of oxblood. Elizabeth looked down at herself to see the same color scheme reflected by her leather leggings and deep red tank top.

"Please don't be Alice," she said under her breath, as the being inside the chrysalis began to emerge. "Or a snake."

When the last seam of the chrysalis tore and fell down to the earth, a blue butterfly emerged. It was nearly as big as Elizabeth. It floated softly down to a branch beside her near the edge of the clearing, and stood there watching her as curiously as she was watching it, reflecting her nature in a way that made her shift her weight back and forth between her black soles.

"Hello?" Elizabeth called out softly.

The butterfly stared back at her, flapping his large blue wings slowly. Amongst the blue, there was a pattern of black dots. The wings mirrored each another with perfect symmetry, making the two black circles at the tip of each wing look like dead eyes staring down at her, as the butterfly lowered his wings.

"Hello!" Elizabeth called louder. "Don't be scared."

"Hello," the butterfly replied, though she couldn't see where his voice came from. He watched her and flapped his broad wings gingerly.

"I'm Elizabeth, I'm just a girl."

"If you think that's all you are, you might want to look in a mirror."

"That's nice of you," she replied, as she scratched the back of her neck. "It's just that I saw you come out of your chrysalis, and I have to say, I thought it was beautiful. So beautiful that I forgot what I was doing in the forest for a second. I'm looking for someone, a girl like me. Actually, she's not really like me at all. She's wearing a blue dress like the blue on your wings—"

"How easy it is to forget that while we spend our time chasing the light, the darkness spends its time chasing us," the butterfly interrupted, as he flew to a thick branch closer to Elizabeth.

"I don't think she's anything like a light," she said, as she scratched the inside of her wrist. "Honestly, I think she's the opposite."

"Nothing here is what it appears to be. But rest assured, you most certainly are searching for light. We all chase the light, whether we're awake or asleep."

There was something about the butterfly's voice that felt rich, like those sticky summer mornings that make the world move slowly. From the wide branch where he rested, he observed her every movement, as if she were a painting that had just come to life. For a moment, Elizabeth's eyes fell to the red scratch marks on her right wrist, and the vision of Mack's tattoo flashed across her mind.

"You remind me of someone. But not someone in Wonderland," she said. She clenched her jaw.

"Is he a butterfly too? As you witnessed earlier, I haven't always been a butterfly."

Just when she was about to open her mouth, she was interrupted by another image. This time the vision was of Alice.

"Can I ask you something?" she continued. "You say you haven't always been a butterfly. Are you the caterpillar? The one who met Alice?"

The butterfly stopped beating its wings for a moment. "I am nobody. I just am. What I was I am no longer. What I am, you also are."

"Look," Elizabeth said, as she smoothed down the bottom of her shirt. "I'm not good at riddles, alright? I don't know what you mean. I'm not a butterfly."

"Neither am I. I'm made up of the same things as you are. I'm made of the sun and the earth, of the stardust that litters the sky, and of the wicked hearts of men."

"I think we're not seeing eye to eye . . . eyes," she swallowed. "How is it that I feel like we exist in two separate realities simultaneously? Like you're in an altered state," she asked.

"What reality would you like to be in?"

The butterfly's question hit her like a splash of cold water.

"That's a tough one," she replied. "I can't say, because I'm not sure which one I'm in now, or which one I was in before I started meditating. All I know is that I want to be in whichever state can help me understand Wonderland. I want to connect with the other creatures here, because so far I've managed to successfully alienate myself from everyone. The only connection I've made here was with a cat who might actually be insane. So yes," Elizabeth paused, catching her breath. "Being in another reality might suit me better."

After she caught her breath, she watched the butterfly fly down to the ground and land by her feet on top of the remains of his chrysalis. Suddenly he flapped his wings feverishly, and his body shuddered.

"Are you okay?"

His wings flapped so fast that Elizabeth's hair blew behind her shoulders, though she couldn't feel the breeze. His large body vibrated in a blur of black and blue, until finally he stopped abruptly, both wings closed in a triangle over his head. He lowered his wings slowly to reveal an orange pill and a blue pill, one resting on each wing. There were no numbers stamped on their faces.

"Are those—"

"One will speed up the reality around you, and one will slow it down."

"What difference would it make if it's fast or slow?"

"If you alter the reality around you, is it not a new reality? You want a new reality, right?" His voice was rough, like sandpaper.

"I guess, if it will help me find Alice," she said as she bit her lip. "I'm not getting anywhere on my own. Which one is which?"

"Does it matter?"

"I should think so, doesn't it?" she stammered. She looked at the butterfly resting at her feet. The spots on his wings changed, making the eyes look like slits. She wiped her palms on her thighs and looked at the pills. After a moment, she reached down and picked up the blue pill from the butterfly's wing, examining it between her fingers like a diamond. "It doesn't have the number stamped on the front, so how can I be sure this pill is the same as the ones at home?"

"Are you going to take it or not?"

"Just a second," she said, as she turned over the pill in her glistening palm. If the butterfly used it to morph into something beautiful, she thought, something with direction and an infallible sense of self, maybe it could transform her as well. She hoped that she, too, could grow wings.

"Just one lick ought to do it," the butterfly said.

She took a breath.

"Come on, already! What are you waiting for?"

She followed the butterfly's instructions and licked the small surface where the *10* ought to be. Then she dropped it and watched it vanish before it hit the grass. The butterfly flew back to the branch next to her, watching her from above, as if she were beneath a magnifying glass.

I am strong. I am strong and in control.

"Am I a girl in a meditation visualizing a butterfly?" she asked. "Or are you in your own meditation visualizing me? Who is the creation, and who is the creator? In her letter, Alice said the creator is me."

"Listen to the girl in the blue dress," he said in a way that made her feel it was a warning. The roughness of his voice hit her again. It was like swallowing salt water, leaving the back of her throat hoarse. His wings shuddered as he spread them once more. "We must never be intimidated by our own mind. What intimidates you controls you. What we are on the inside and what we are on the outside are one. When you no longer perceive the woods as hostile, then fear cannot linger here. Only surrender can give you what you're looking for."

"But—"

"Didn't you hear what I said? Now get out of here!"

She blinked and saw blue ink on a scarred wrist and felt cold night air on the back of her neck as her hands shook. The crinkling of a plastic bag faded into the darkness. A tall, skinny man disappeared into the night. She blinked again and saw the butterfly leap into the air. His wings pushed off with such force that her hair blew off of her neck. He flew beyond the trees, taking the orange pill with him.

Suddenly, Elizabeth felt things begin to slow down around her, as if with each step she took her feet kissed the earth. The butterfly's last words slid off her shoulders like thick molasses, leaving her lighter, with each footstep bouncing off the ground a little higher. She wondered what he evolved into before he flew away, leaving her with nothing but her heartbeat and the slowing murmurs of her thoughts.

"What am I really looking for?" she asked herself. Her legs moved forward as if she were walking through mud. She knew she was looking for Alice, the infamous girl in the blue dress who struck fear in every creature she met, but only in the hopes that she would have answers. "Maybe it's like the butterfly said. I'm just looking for the truth."

As she continued through the clearing and into the forest, the metamorphosis of her own reality unfolded before her eyes. She touched each branch and each leaf with the awareness that she touched the whole of Wonderland. Finding a fallen log, she sat and let her thoughts do the walking. She traced her fingers along the bark beneath her, around its labyrinth of ridges, like the wrath and mire of human veins. She saw herself running along each corridor, like an ant would, running in circles, only to retrace her steps.

I am strong. I am strong and in control.

The trunk's broad surface looked inviting. Elizabeth lowered her back down on its spine and looked up at the washed-out Wonderland sky. She longed to fall into it, to be absorbed by it—the way she wanted to become a part of Adam before she fell down the rabbit hole. She wanted to escape herself and become a part of something bigger, something more whole. She ached to fit together with something that made her feel as if she could fall upwards, the way she felt when she looked into Adam's eyes—forest green with a blackness in the middle like the branches that jutted out above her. She wanted to fall into the sky and emerge on the other side, landing right in Adam's arms, sturdy like the trunk beneath her.

Memories of him rushed at her all at once, but got stuck before they could reach her—limbless specters, beautiful, strong, and strange.

She was unsure of how long she idled, but finally a thought entered her mind that she couldn't shake.

Where's Alice?

She clenched her jaw and sat up, pushing her hair out of her face and tucking a wild strand behind her ear. The thought flew away from her, and she was left with a deafening, existential "now what." She took a long inhale.

Suddenly, Wonderland stood still, and she received an

image in her mind that she had almost forgotten: the Cheshire Cat.

If you should need me, simply think of me and ask. His words flashed through her mind as quickly as his face had vanished.

"Cheshire," Elizabeth pleaded. "I need help."

Silence.

"I need you!" she said louder, yelling her words to the treetops.

Closing her eyes, Elizabeth envisioned the Cheshire Cat before her. She felt the relief of recognizing his orange body floating in front of her. Peace grabbed Doubt and Worry by the collars and pushed them back into the nothingness from whence they came.

But her visualization was cut short by a familiar, deranged laugh.

"Looking for this?" the Cheshire Cat said with amusement. His long, orange tail was wrapped around a branch a few feet in front of her, and he dangled with glee as his satanic grin widened to frame two glistening fangs. In his right paw he held a folded piece of paper with jagged and torn edges.

"Cheshire Cat!" Elizabeth said with a smile so wide she felt a pinch in her cheeks. "I asked for you to come, and you came!"

He took a bow, keeping his grin wide and fixed.

I've never been so happy to see a crazy person in my life.

"Even madmen keep their promises, my dear," the Cat laughed deeply. His laughter then turned into hysteria, and he began to vanish as quickly as he had appeared. When he was completely gone, his laughter could still be heard, echoing against the wall of trees around her. The letter he held in his paw floated to the ground with the grace of a butterfly.

"Wait—"

The Cheshire Cat's laughter dissipated, and she was left alone with only her thoughts and the letter he left behind.

"I should really try to keep my thoughts more discreet," Elizabeth scolded herself as she grabbed the letter.

Quickly, her fingers danced across its surface, frantically unfolding its ragged seams. It appeared the paper had undergone as difficult a journey through the woods as she had. She looked worn and jagged herself. As the final fold came undone, she read the letter with the familiar curly script.

You should know you look incredibly stupid, running around in circles.

If you look just behind you, you'll notice the Wonderland gate. Your descent into altered realities—distractions really— brought you right back to the start. Did you have fun chasing your tail?

This whole time you thought those pills made your thoughts go away—the thoughts that taunt you like demons, the ones that attack you in the morning and tell you to look in the mirror. Newsflash, bitch, they didn't quiet down. They didn't go anywhere. They want you to find me, that's why they led you down here! When you sat down on that dirty old mat to meditate, you thought the pill was wearing off, and that that's why those pesky thoughts came back again. The truth is that you listened to the serpent, you followed it down the rabbit hole, and now you're here.

That's right, I'm talking about the snake inside you. That bird saw right through you, and so do I.

For the record, there's nothing strong or "in control" about you.

Have you forgotten that I'm still waiting? I'll wait for you until your body turns to ash and you begin your search for me again—in this reality or another.

But seriously, I can't believe you trusted a butterfly over me. Do you take candy from every dealer on the street? Are you that pathetic? I wonder how Mack would feel about you taking your business elsewhere. Or, better yet, I wonder how Adam would feel about your dirty little habit in the first place.

But the butterfly did have one thing right, you know. You really should look in a mirror.

—Alice

Six

Elizabeth ripped the letter in half and shoved the slivers into her back pocket with the others.

"But how?" she asked, as her voice cracked.

She wondered a million things all at once, each thought raising its hand to try and win her attention. She wondered if Alice could expose her to Adam and how she knew Mack. She bit the inside of her cheek. The thought that won her affection was the tiniest one, the lingering gnawing of Alice's identity and the scope of her power. The feeling of looking at herself through a microscope, exposed and bare, shining a light in the darkest labyrinths of her heart.

She looked up at the sky again. It was streaked with the black branches of trees looming high above her. They stood out more prominently against their opaque backdrop than they had against the sky in the clearing. The branches that once entwined like tangled corridors now looked like thick, bony fingers. She recognized that in the heart of Wonderland, phantasmal monsters and friends both awaited her, and the sky darkened as she continued her journey inward.

Her pulse began to quicken at the thought of going back into the darkness. She took a few steps back and reached out for the log, her white knuckles gleaming against its black surface. It caught her as she nearly tripped over an overturned root. She let her nails grip the bark, strong and sturdy. Then Adam's face cut into the darkness of her mind, and she imagined her long nails sneaking underneath his shirt, sliding across his skin.

Does he know where I am? she asked herself. She smiled at the thought of him there next to her, pointing out which path to follow and rolling his eyes at her lack of direction. He always knew where he was going. She liked that about him. One of the first times they spoke in high school was when he showed her a shortcut to the gym, avoiding the busiest hallways that always swallowed her whole. He was one of those men with an internal compass, the type of man who chooses a woman who is either his true north or his fleeting detour. Ever since they met Elizabeth strived to be the former.

Despite him not being there with her, when she thought of him she felt him very close to her soul, as if they were simply two halves of a whole. She felt her heart beating in her chest as she slowly let go of the fallen trunk. She felt as if each beat of her heart tapped out a sort of Morse code that spelled out his name, calling to him.

What am I going to tell him when I get back? she asked herself. *If I get back?*

Elizabeth began to feel the weight of her last thought on her shoulders. The only certainty she had in this moment was that she needed to find Alice. She imagined Alice plotting against her somewhere in the dark madness of Wonderland. Her shoulders began to ache, as did the familiar spot between her eyebrows. In a desperate attempt to escape her own thoughts, which ricocheted between Alice and Adam, between fear and comfort, she chose to give life to a memory of Adam. She thought back to the morning, right before she rolled out of bed to begin her morning routine. She recalled the warmth of his body next to hers, and she felt Fitz's square body nestled in the folds of the blanket by their feet. She awoke before Adam, resting her head on his chest, and noticed that their hearts beat in sync. She heard the beat in her mind so clearly that she began to feel it in her body. For a moment, it was as if she had two heartbeats, and in that instant, she became numb to the fear she felt in this place, like the butterfly had told her. In her heart and within her mind's eye she was with Adam once more, in a Wonderland of their own.

She walked forward to the melody of branches and leaves crunching beneath her feet. Leaves to ash, then ash to soil, repeating until the Earth took its last breath.

The smell of sweet decay lingered, but it reminded her of life instead of death, of a world that had the courage to begin again, of a soul that could shed its leaves without the fear of becoming nothing. She walked with the specter of Adam guiding her among the trees, standing tributes to perpetual destruction and rebirth, and she felt at home. Just for a moment.

She held fast to this connection, following her new route and turning a sharp corner, when a scene took form before her that made her stop in her tracks.

Before her, she recognized the twin faces, both strange and yet familiar, of Tweedle Dee and Tweedle Dum.

The twin brothers stood facing each other under a tall willow tree. The strange thing about these identical twins was that they were hardly identical at all. They both wore a shirt with a striped pattern that mirrored the other's, with the twin on the left having black stripes where the other's stripes were white. Over their striped shirts, one Tweedle twin wore black overalls while the other wore white. The left corner of the collar of the twin on the right stood straight up, whereas the right corner of the collar on the twin on the left stood tall. The spinners on top of their hats spun in opposite directions, even though she didn't feel any breeze that would make them spin at all.

As one looked into the eyes of the other he would smooth out his hair or remove a piece of dust from his eye, and the other twin would mirror his twin's action on the opposite side of his face. One was the other's opposite but equal reflection brought to life in human form.

She approached the twins carefully, coming within five feet of them before she stopped. At first, she thought they didn't notice her, as they seemed completely preoccupied with their own appearance, until she stepped on a loose twig that snapped loudly and both twins turned to face her.

"He says hello," remarked the twin on the right. He stood in perfect symmetry to his twin next to him, the way one half of a snowflake reflects the other.

"Hello," she said, "Are you—"

"SHHHH!" the twin on the left interrupted.

"Sorry," Elizabeth whispered, unsure of why she had to be quiet but obliging the twins all the same, so as to avoid giving a bad impression. "Are you Tweedle Dee?"

"Yes," whispered the twin on the right.

"You are?" Elizabeth said, turning to him.

"He says yes, he's Tweedle Dee," the twin on the right said in clarification.

"Alright, so that makes you Tweedle Dum?"

"He says yes," Tweedle Dee said, speaking for his brother.

"Glad to meet you both," she said. "Why are we whispering?"

"You're going to wake up the tree!" cried Tweedle Dee softly. The willow tree behind them was still, its limbs descending to the floor in a waterfall of leaves and twisting branches.

"Wake him?" Elizabeth whispered. "Trees sleep?"

"Of course they sleep, don't you?" both twins spoke softly at once. She wondered if they thought the same thing at the same time, each speaking for and mimicking the other.

She studied the tree for a moment, crossing and uncrossing her arms as she stood before it. The tree looked like a normal tree to her, sleeping or otherwise.

"What happens if the tree wakes up?"

Tweedle Dum gasped.

"Hmm?" she prodded.

"He says we would all vanish, of course," Tweedle Dee said.

"Vanish? Why?"

"Because we're all parts of his dream, silly."

"Me? I just got here," Elizabeth said, folding her arms tightly across her chest.

"You think you're real, don't you?" Tweedle Dee continued, placing his left hand on his cheek thoughtfully. His brother stood silently next to him and placed his right hand on his opposite cheek.

"Of course I'm real!"

"SHHHH!" Tweedle Dum interjected, removing his hand from his cheek and putting his index finger over his lips, which his brother mimicked with his opposite hand.

"Sorry," Elizabeth mumbled, as she rolled her eyes. "But how do you know that I'm not the one who's actually sleeping, and that it's you two who are parts of my dream? For all you know, I could be the one who created this place! How do you know if I have or not?"

"Because you're already half-awake," Tweedle Dee said softly, itching his nose at the same time as his brother, but with the opposite hand on the opposite nostril.

"But that doesn't make any sense," Elizabeth said, folding her arms more tightly to her chest. "How could you possibly know if I'm awake? And how can someone be only half-awake?"

"Because you've awakened to your purpose, haven't you? Yet you're still asleep while you're acting it out. Have you got a purpose?"

"Yes," she said, "I have to get out of Wonderland, and to do that I have to find someone who I think is trying to kill me, but—"

"Then you've woken up within the dream. You're both awake and dreaming. You're creating everything around you and playing out your own dream all at once," Tweedle Dum said quietly. "And so we couldn't possibly vanish, not all at once anyway. Isn't it wonderful!"

"I'm not dreaming," she said as she rolled her eyes. "I was meditating when I came here."

"Dreaming, meditating, what's the difference?" Tweedle Dee whispered back.

"While the tree is sleeping, it doesn't know it's dreaming," Tweedle Dum continued. "But when it wakes up it'll know. When we all wake up we'll know that this place is like a dream."

"That's logic," the brothers agreed in a whisper.

"Are you both telepathic? Or do you just mirror each other's thoughts?" she asked. Her question almost answered itself as the twins turned to face one another again, with one twin scratching his left eye and the other scratching his right. "For example, whose eye was itching just now?"

"His!" both brothers exclaimed, pointing to one another with opposite arms in accusation.

"Why don't you each just look in a mirror instead of using each other?"

"Why use a mirror when you can just look at your twin!"

Adam flashed through her mind for a moment, his smiling face and green eyes shining through her consciousness like a lighthouse guiding her home, igniting the familiar dancing butterflies in her stomach. The feeling disappeared as quickly as it came, but it was a welcome light in a dark place.

"I don't have a twin," Elizabeth said. Tears welled up in her eyes, as the thought of Adam faded from her mind. One spilled over and ran down her cheek.

"He says don't cry!" Tweedle Dum said. "We all have a twin!"

Elizabeth wiped her cheek, but she felt no wetness.

"If you want to use a mirror yourself, I suppose you could borrow this one," Tweedle Dee said, as Tweedle Dum rolled out an ornate mirror from behind the willow tree, hidden by the broad trunk. "We never use it, anyway!"

"No thanks, I'm fine. I don't need to do that," Elizabeth said, holding her arms out in front of her. "I'll just ask you for some directions and then be on my way."

Her old companions, Doubt and Worry, joined hands and danced in circles around her mind.

"Are you sure? I have no use for it, I can just look at him!" the twins said at once, pointing to one another again with opposite arms.

"Yes, I'm sure. Thanks. I need to know if you saw the girl I'm looking for. She's wearing a blue dress, her name is Alice, maybe you know her—"

"Here you are, come closer!" The twins walked toward her, closing the gap between them inch by inch. Tweedle Dum carried the mirror in his arms, struggling under its weight and wide, gothic frame, as Tweedle Dee grunted with fatigue.

Elizabeth stared at the twins holding the mirror. She wiped her sweaty palms on her pants, leaving wet tracks on the leather. The mirror flashed in the light, its dark frame beckoning her forward.

"You're not listening to me," she whispered.

They continued to struggle with the mirror as they inched closer.

"I don't need to see it," Elizabeth said hurriedly, holding out her arms in protest. "I just need to know what direction Alice went!"

"Help me hold it!" Tweedle Dee whispered in irritation, speaking for his brother who was still struggling with the mirror.

"I've got this corner, now prop it up on my back so she can see properly. She's tall," Tweedle Dee barked, embodying his brother's struggle. They had almost stood the mirror high enough upon Tweedle Dum's back for Elizabeth to see herself.

"No!" she screamed, her voice booming against the willow tree and the other trees that surrounded her and the twins.

Suddenly, Tweedle Dee and Tweedle Dum vanished, a horror-stricken expression still frozen on their faces. The large mirror came crashing to the forest floor, breaking into a million shards of glass at Elizabeth's feet. As soon as they touched the grass, the splinters turned to ash.

She called out the twins' names several times, but her calls were met with silence.

"This can't be happening," she panted, the space between her temples throbbing.

She ran past the willow tree into the darkness of the forest. The low boughs of the black trees around her began to reach and tear at her shirt and leggings, scratching her bare arms and pulling at her hair. They snagged the stitches in the pattern on her back pockets, ripping at the white threads. The branches slowed her down, but her heart was beating frantically. She was trying to outrun her claustrophobia, which set in quickly, despite her being in a forest that seemed infinite in all directions.

She thought of how Adam used to joke that she was "the mother of the wounded," compassionate for the under-dog and those who suffered, yet she tore herself apart from the inside.

She continued to run, jumping over fallen branches.

She had been friendly to every creature in Wonderland so far, even if they hadn't been friendly back. She remembered Adam telling her to be kind to herself the way she is to others, but that felt backward. She remembered the Golden Rule working the other way around. The image of the mirror in her bathroom floated through her mind, and Adam staring at her with those big green eyes that made her want to be better. She thought about the strain in Tweedle Dum's back, how the mirror cut into his spine. She thought of his brother primping himself. She thought of the look of horror on their faces before they disappeared. The folds in their skin deepened, a black shadow cast across their faces.

She wondered if she killed them, or if they were alive now, somewhere, in some parallel universe, some parallel Wonderland. Somewhere else, someone else could be meditating, some other girl in some other part of the world, and maybe she would see them appear.

"Someone more compassionate and braver than me," she said between deep inhales.

Just then, a tree branch hit her right in her chest, knocking the wind out of her. She laid flat on her back, the salt of her welling tears stinging her eyes, pricking them like the rough branches that grazed her skin. Her lungs felt empty. She took handfuls of leaves and ash into her fists, as she pushed herself upright.

She had to stop running. The guilt and the thickening branches obstructed her path, a jury of trees staring down at her to keep her from running away. Had she been left with Doubt and Worry conducting her thoughts like demonic maestros, they would have beaten her until she couldn't stand. If the outside was truly a reflection of the inside, Elizabeth felt a part of her begin to vanish, as if another layer peeled off and left her with new, dewy skin, naked and exposed, black ash beneath her fingernails.

The low hanging branches suddenly narrowed until they formed a natural gate. She entered the gate and then came to a halt in front of a thick wall of branches that was impossible to penetrate. In the middle of one of the branches sticking out in front of her, almost touching her nose, was a small, thin sheet of paper. It was fastened with a small white thread, just like the threads from Elizabeth's back pocket.

As Elizabeth opened the note, her fingertips were stained black from the ink that was still wet.

I know what you did. I saw the look in their eyes.

You're a murderer.

You killed the truth in cold blood. Even when it's right in front of you, staring you in the face. And when it comes to the truth you never stare back. Not for long.

Is that why you can't look at yourself in the mirror? I'll tell you what I see: I see a terrified little girl trapped inside an illusion of yourself that you created, too frightened to break free. The truth is that you don't want to know what lies beyond the looking glass.

The Tweedles only wanted you to look at yourself. And you killed them. Is Adam next?

I'm a killer, too, you know.

You know what you have to do now, princess. And this time don't be so weak. Cowardice was never a good look on you.

Go back. You can fix it.

— Alice

When Elizabeth looked up from the note, she saw that the wall of trees had transformed into a wall of stones.

"But I'm not a killer," Elizabeth said to herself.

She bit her lip and kicked a fallen branch. Her old friends, Doubt and Worry, whispered in her ears and stroked her hair.

She wondered if Alice would be waiting for her when she got back to the willow tree, her blue dress muddied and ripped, with a twisted smile plastered across her face and murder in her eyes. She wondered if Alice had been behind the willow tree the whole time. Maybe she handed Tweedle Dum the mirror.

A prickling sensation ran up Elizabeth's arms, and she wondered if Alice was always watching.

Seven

$\mathcal{E}$lizabeth retraced her steps back to the willow tree. When she closed her eyes, she could feel the trees bending in toward her again, tugging at her hair and scraping her skin. But when she opened her eyes, she saw nothing but open space and her own tracks zigzagging through the fallen leaves. With each odd step she took, she felt the crunching paper in her back pocket, as if Alice whispered a quiet threat to keep moving.

Murderer. The word entered her mind and the back of her throat grew dry.

"I didn't know they would vanish," she pleaded to herself. "How could I have known that?"

Her question was answered only by the rustling of leaves and her heavy footfalls.

Murderer. The word tasted salty on her tongue and felt heavy on her heart. She opened her mouth to take in the cold, refreshing air—air that could make the feeling stop— but instead she let out a sob of a woman cracking into girl-sized pieces.

For a moment, she was no longer the woman who inno-cently forgot to hang up her shirts for work but could remember her parents' anniversary. She wasn't the woman with the crumpled receipts, beat-up aviator sunglasses, and hair ties that disappeared into a murky void at the bottom of her handbag, who surprised her boyfriend with new shoes on his birthday. She wasn't her bachelor's degree hanging on the wall of her parents' house, or her on-time rent payments. She wasn't the girl with good intentions who made mistakes. She was a murderer. A girl out of control.

Shut up and breathe, she pleaded with herself.

More leaves crunched beneath her feet.

Is Alice capable of hurting Adam? she thought.

The thought dangled in her mind like a spider building its web, her heart dangling with it. Each thread tied together with the images flashing in her mind, a slideshow of horrors projected by Doubt and Worry. Alice and Adam. Adam disappearing. Alice waiting for her in their apartment. Sticky thread tied neatly in a bow, entrapping her sense of hope in its wicked snare.

It took her one long minute of courage and concentration to find her breath, and to find silence from the avalanche of thoughts that Doubt and Worry had sent crashing over the craggy cliffs of her mind. Yet in the silence, she still heard a faint scratching at her door as Doubt and Worry looked for a way back in.

"There's no way I'm going to let Alice touch Adam," she said as she looked around her. "I hope you can hear me, Alice! You'll never touch him. In reality, in a meditation, in a dream, or anywhere else for that matter."

She felt that somehow, somewhere, Alice could hear her.

Alice was the magnetic center, the true north around which Wonderland revolved. She had a connection to the place that allowed it to see and know her every move, even before she knew it herself. But there was something to that voice, her intensity. There was something deceiving in the blue of her dress, which camouflaged the fire raging within her, a fire Elizabeth felt she could touch. A blue flame that mirrored her own. If she was capable of anything, she could be capable of getting to Adam. Finally, the thought that clawed at the back of Elizabeth's dry throat leapt out into the cool forest air.

"Over my dead body," she murmured to herself.

The forked trees whispered around her, muffled, as if someone spoke behind a shielded hand. Her stomach turned over. She was nearing the willow tree when a barrage of thoughts came into her mind and slowed her down, as if she were trudging through waist-deep mud. She wondered if the Tweedles would be standing there, or if it would be like one of those moments one always prayed for with burning cheeks, begging that a scene would replay itself from the beginning, from before your failure, like the world had stopped and nothing had ever happened and you were clean again. She wondered if Alice had the power to control time, or if it was time that had the power to control us. The Tweedles wanted her to see herself, to confront herself in a way that made her vulnerable. She blinked and saw the mirror crash again in her mind.

Suddenly, Elizabeth's thoughts were interrupted by the sound of something rolling through the leafy floor, headed straight for her. Already on edge, she jumped to the side only to see a half-peeled onion roll past her and come to rest at the bottom of a broad tree trunk.

"Catch!" a giggling voice called from nowhere in particular.

Then, just as suddenly as the appearance of the onion, the laughter materialized. Resting in between a fork in the tree trunk above the onion was the familiar orange face of the Cheshire Cat, giggling louder and louder in his dark, demented way.

"You were supposed to catch it," the Cat said with a crooked grin.

"Catch it? You scared me to death!"

"Don't be mad at the onion, it doesn't know how to roll backwards!"

"I promise you, it's not the onion I'm mad at. Why did you throw it in the first place?" she panted. "And what's it doing here?"

"It's your ego, of course! What does it look like?"

"It looks like an onion to me."

"Po-tay-toe, po-TAH-toe!" he enunciated with a screech. "You don't remember what I told you before? Nothing here is as it appears to be." The rest of his body slowly took form. The Cat scooped up the tattered onion with his tail and brought it to his nose. As he sniffed it, his face contorted at the putrid scent emanating from its exposed, unpeeled innards.

"What are you trying to say? That I peeled back another layer?"

"Now we're getting somewhere!" he said, as the onion disappeared from his tail's grip. Only its sour scent lingered.

"If I peeled the first layer back at the meadow courtyard, the surface layer with all of those superficial thoughts," Elizabeth reasoned, more to herself than the Cat. "And then I peeled away the self-destructive layer, with the cheap distractions the butterfly gave me, then this layer has to be something a little deeper, right?"

As she spoke, the Cheshire Cat became preoccupied with himself, balancing a stray twig on his orange-patterned forehead.

"Can you pay attention? I'm trying to figure this out," she continued. "How many layers are left?"

"That depends," the Cat replied, as the stick turned into a green butterfly and promptly floated away. "Is it just me, or do I sense it's getting darker?"

"Darker? Yes, I noticed that already," she said with irritation. "That's why I want to find Alice before nightfall. But what does that have to do with layers?" She watched as the Cat tried to swat after the retreating butterfly with his paw, causing him to lose his balance and nearly fall from the tree. "Anyway, I thought you said you would only come if I called you? I wasn't thinking of you at all!"

"I have a mind of my own, you know," the Cat replied through thick spells of laughter, as he dug his claws into the tree trunk for support. "Do you?"

"Of course I do," she groaned.

"You could have fooled me!" the Cheshire Cat mused in his own broken laughter, as he jumped from branch to branch around Elizabeth.

"Great, I'm glad I'm such a joke to you," Elizabeth said,

as she folded her arms across her chest. "Now leave. I think I know the way this time. Like you said, it's getting darker and I'm heading back to the willow tree to find the Tweedle twins."

"Look who finally knows the way!" he choked out, and then he laughed so hard that he hiccupped. "But do you know the way once you're there?"

His question was the one thought that Doubt and Worry left out of their chorus.

"No, I guess not," Elizabeth said. She glanced over her shoulder to face him again. *To be honest I'm not sure what I need to fix when I get back there,* she said to herself instead of speaking aloud. *Or exactly what I missed the first time I was there. They told me the willow tree had been asleep, but I think I was the one who was asleep the whole time.*

"No, no, no! That won't do!" the Cheshire Cat interjected, listening to the thoughts in her head, "If you want to know where you're going, it won't help you to look back and worry. You must look forward!" he continued, as his head spun around wildly on his neck, making a full turn.

"Spare me your motivational pep talks, alright? You don't have to eavesdrop on my thoughts, you could have just asked me to speak for myself," she snapped.

They stared at each other for a moment.

"Fine. Maybe you're right. So far, worrying has only led me further into the darkness."

"Just like Wonderland."

"What?"

"It's simple, really. The deeper you go, the darker it gets," the Cheshire Cat said, and for a moment Elizabeth swore she saw Alice's blue eyes in place of the Cat's. "Do you not feel the quiet beat of the heart of darkness growing closer? You know you're headed straight for it, at the rate you're going. The outside is just a reflection of the inside."

She blinked and his eyes were his own again, and he sat licking his paws, as if he hadn't said a word. She felt pulses run through her body as her synapses fired all at once, and then hardly at all.

"Anyway, it was overcast when you saw the first layer peel away, the one at the meadow courtyard. Then it grew darker and darker as you went along," the Cheshire Cat said, as he looked up at her from his paws. "The blue pill had you quite lost, when you left the butterfly—I'll give you a hint, never trust anything that doesn't have to flap its wings to fly—and then just as you are about to see yourself, you caused the Tweedles to disappear!" With this, the Cat broke into a deep purr, "How prrredictable!"

She looked down at her feet.

"In her note, Alice said to fix this. I heard the words you read," the Cheshire Cat mused. "Tweedle Dee and Tweedle Dum just wanted to connect with you, to show you yourself. Sure, they were a little vain. But aren't we all?" He ran his sandpaper tongue over his paw and stroked his forehead, smoothing the orange pattern between his eyes, "Now, be a good girl, repay them properly!"

Then his whiskers began to twitch, and he faded away in an orange haze that left Elizabeth completely alone with her thoughts again. An infinite amount of choices and possibilities hung like baubles on the willow tree ahead of her.

I can fix this. I know I can, she thought to herself. She took a deep breath and resolved to coax out the fears, Doubt and Worry, that hid behind her ribs. She told herself to be in the moment, to connect with her breath. *I may not be ready to see myself, but maybe I can get the twins to find that ability for themselves.* She thought that if they could learn to look beyond their own looks, then maybe they could speak for themselves instead of speaking for one another.

She felt her breath flowing through her body. She let it fill her up, like a child would blow up a balloon until it popped, creating lightness in her step where the mud had once held her back. She drifted easily through the forest like the Cheshire Cat. She was the red balloon, wide with invisible hope. She was the onion rolling silently through the leaves.

She closed her eyes and began to visualize the Tweedles standing beneath the tree, happily grooming themselves in the reflection of the other, whispering to one another idly so as to avoid waking the tree behind them. She made sure to imagine a distinct, empty piece of grass behind the willow tree.

When she opened her eyes, she saw herself standing before that very scene. Tweedle Dee and Tweedle Dum stood beneath the sleeping willow, fixing themselves up in the other's reflection. Tweedle Dee patted down the right side of his collar, smoothing it down, and Tweedle Dum proceeded to do the same to the left side of his collar, though it had mysteriously flattened on its own. Their narcissism remained palpably the same, but Elizabeth's voice was strong.

"Hello," whispered Elizabeth, careful not to wake the tree behind them.

Tweedle Dum and Tweedle Dee turned to face her, again in perfect symmetry. "What did you say?" Tweedle Dum asked softly. "He couldn't hear you."

"I said hello. I'm Elizabeth."

"Pleasure," they whispered at once, offering her opposite hands.

At first she was cautious to shake their hands as the distant, foggy memory of whimsical songs, poems, and dancing floated through her mind. To her relief, after a small squeeze they withdrew their hands.

"I thought you were both fond of dancing, nonsensical poetry, and other things?" Elizabeth asked, wearily. The twins had gone back to grooming themselves.

"It takes work to look like this, you know," Tweedle Dee said on behalf of his brother, who was mouthing the words without saying them. "Who has time to recite tales about walruses all day long?"

Elizabeth paused for a moment, glancing around for Alice.

"There it is!" said Tweedle Dee.

"Who?" she asked hurriedly.

"You have a spot! Just there, under your eye!" Tweedle Dee whispered discreetly to Elizabeth, who had a small mascara track from where a tear slid down her cheek during their last conversation.

Tweedle Dum pointed to his own cheek, "Would you like to see a mirror?"

She heard a familiar voice inside her screaming at her to run. Instead she took a deep breath and felt the lush grass beneath her boots where she stood. It was the same spot where she stood before everything had gone wrong. She wiped furiously at the black smudge on her face and tried to keep her wits about her.

"I have a mirror, actually!" Elizabeth mused, playing along now that she knew the rules. "His name is Adam. He's like my twin," she explained slowly, realizing that she had never said that aloud before. "He shows me myself, my own inner and outer truth, all the time. He's a reflection of myself, only sometimes I can't see it."

"Can't see it!" Tweedle Dee said quietly, as his twin chuckled quietly on his right, clearly thinking the thought that Tweedle Dee had said aloud. "But he's a man, and you're a woman!"

"It's what he shows me that's on the inside that's important," Elizabeth offered. Suddenly, a thought struck her that seemed to materialize out of nowhere. "Can you two see yourselves? Or only one another?"

"Shh!" the Tweedles echoed in a shrilled whisper. "Not so loud! The willow tree is sleeping."

"Right," Elizabeth muttered. She dug the compact out of her pocket and ran her fingers over its smooth, pink-stamped edges.

"Of course we see ourselves," Tweedle Dum said softly. "We were just looking at ourselves!" Tweedle Dee lowered his arms. He had been making gesticulations with his hands while his brother spoke.

"Of course you can," Elizabeth cooed, opening the compact outstretched in front of her.

Tweedle Dum caught his own reflection in the mirror for

a moment and said, "Tweedle Dee, your hair is sticking up on the side!"

Mistaking himself for his brother, Tweedle Dum laughed as he looked at his own reflection. It occurred to Elizabeth that he was seeing himself for the first time. Tweedle Dee stood beside him, struck with utter confusion, as he patted the hair on the sides of his head. Tweedle Dum fixed his own hair and continued to giggle quietly, so as not to wake the tree.

"I have something to say," he announced, finally giving form to his own thoughts instead of his brother's.

"He wants to know why you're here," Tweedle Dee said, cutting his brother off and shooting him a warning glare.

Elizabeth closed the mirror and held it in her palm, happy to have given Tweedle Dum his own voice for a moment, even if the moment was short. "I was thinking—"

"It's a strange sort of mind that only works backwards," Tweedle Dum said for himself again, but without the presence of the compact this time.

"I'm here to make sure that the willow tree remains asleep," Elizabeth said with a smile. "And that I remain fully awake."

"Half-awake!" Tweedle Dum chimed in softly as usual.

"Yes, half-awake. I'm also here to find out which direction a girl named Alice went in. It's very important that I find her. She has blonde hair and is wearing a blue dress, she's about my height—"

"Oh yes, I've seen her!" cried Tweedle Dum. "Your twin!"

As Tweedle Dum spoke, Tweedle Dee looked at him in

anguish, and then in shock when his brother turned and looked straight at him.

"No, she's not my twin, we look like opposites. Did you hear me before? She's blonde. I have black hair," she said as she twisted a few strands between her fingers. "She dresses in blue and I'm wearing red and—"

"How dare you!" Tweedle Dee barked at his brother under his breath. "It's like I'm not even here! You're making me look ridiculous!"

"I'm doing no such thing," Tweedle Dum retorted, looking straight back at him. "You make yourself look ridiculous! Look at you, standing there with a wrinkle in the left shoulder of your overalls!"

Tweedle Dee gasped in disgust, his face turning from red to purple.

"Please, boys, don't fight! If you could just point me in Alice's direction," Elizabeth said calmly.

"She went that way!" both twins responded, pointing in opposite directions with the same arm. Still holding up their arms, they turned to face each other angrily, lost as to how to communicate with the other.

Elizabeth watched with wide eyes as the boys began to circle one another. "Tweedle Dee, Tweedle Dum, please don't turn on each other! You're both handsome and intelligent men!"

Elizabeth's remark fell on deaf ears. The twins continued to circle one another with their fists raised high. Without saying another word, she marched herself into the middle of their duel, as a mother would stand in between her feuding sons.

"Stop! Don't turn on your brother!" Elizabeth said with authority.

"He started it!" cried Tweedle Dee.

"No, it was him!" shot back Tweedle Dum.

"Well, it's a strange sort of mind that only works backwards," Elizabeth said sarcastically.

"I said that!" echoed Tweedle Dum.

"No, I did! Or, I thought it first!" Tweedle Dee said.

"It doesn't matter who said it," Elizabeth said with obvious exasperation, as she stood in between the two boys with her arms outstretched to separate them.

"What does matter is that I know which way Alice went," Tweedle Dee continued, as he glanced at his brother with narrowed eyes.

"She went that way!" Tweedle Dum interjected, pointing to a path behind the willow tree.

"There you go again, taking all the credit! I thought it first!" whined Tweedle Dee.

"It doesn't matter," Elizabeth said, as she rolled her eyes. "Thank you both for telling me. Now please stop trying to fight each other! What happens if one of you takes a swing? Does the other get hurt, or do you just end up hurting yourself?"

The boys lowered their fists and stared at one another with wide eyes.

"A black eye!" Tweedle Dum said quietly, as he covered his mouth with his hand.

"Never!" shouted Tweedle Dee in protest, his shrill voice breaking the silence and waking the willow tree. At that moment, he stepped away from Elizabeth and grabbed his brother, burying his face in his brother's overalls. Then the two began to disappear. They vanished more slowly than they had the first time. Before they were completely out of sight, Elizabeth was sure that she saw the two embracing in a full, warm hug.

Standing alone beneath the willow tree, she knew that wherever the twins were now, they each had their own voice.

Somewhere, they're half-awake, too, Elizabeth thought. *I must be next.*

She scanned her surroundings for any sounds or signs that Alice had been watching. Again she heard nothing, and so she turned her attention to the path before her. The Cheshire Cat's face flashed through her mind. She knew the only way to go was forward.

Elizabeth ran her hands down the tree trunk, looking for a note from Alice, but to her surprise, there was nothing to be found.

"I don't need Alice's approval," she said to herself with a smile. "I have my own."

Yet she longed to find the girl in the blue dress.

Eight

Elizabeth nibbled at the inside of her cheek, unsure if the sound of her footsteps were really her own. Alice's silence didn't mean she wasn't there. For all Elizabeth knew, she was walking blindly into a trap.

After she walked a ways from the willow tree, she turned around to see it once more, but it had vanished. She was unsure if the tree had run off, or if it had been a part of a dream within her meditation, but she knew it served its purpose. The thought of things no longer needed simply disappearing was freeing. She usually carried the weight of them on her shoulders. Vanishing no longer worried her. The Tweedles and the tree disappearing felt like a beautiful earthquake, a cracked hourglass with sand spilling from the tree bark through the spaces between their ribs. They made her feel locked in time and space, whole and eternal.

Years of meditation had made her sure of herself and her surroundings in the world she was familiar with, but in Wonderland, everything was uncertain and unpredictable. She found a strange comfort in that. Here, with every step she took, she wrote the lines of her life story. In Wonderland, she was the author of her own life, and the Cheshire Cat, as insane as he seemed, knew that the external world reflected the internal world.

"And one more thing is predictable here," she said to herself, as she gazed down at her feet and took a breath. She could barely see her shadow. Each step led her further into the darkness, as if her faint outline was a ghost existing halfway between here and there. The sky that was once a grayish blue, like the sky after the passing of a storm, had dissolved into twilight. The darkness was threatening. "There's no way time exists here," Elizabeth said to herself, as she walked along the path, wondering to herself what lies at the heart of it all, "So how does it get darker?"

She wondered if she had been in Wonderland for days, and if she could ever know that without the presence of the sun or moon. All she knew for certain was that it was longer than the ten minutes she originally intended when she sat down to meditate.

The path she treaded was less difficult than the one she had walked along after Tweedle Dee and Tweedle Dum vanished for the first time. There was much less debris and thick branches. To her surprise, whenever she encountered a branch or a weed in her way, it would simply roll, slide, walk, or slither out of her way, the way a Mome Rath would.

To Elizabeth, the flora and fauna in Wonderland were much more polite than the people at home. She remembered how the crowds pushed through her on the busy New York City streets she called home.

Then, there it was again, the sudden thought that tried

to claw its way out of her but got stuck in her throat—the thought of home, and home meant Adam.

The feeling that she was separated from him and from everyone around her overtook her, and she felt the sensation of needing to swallow constantly. She thought of how she felt before Wonderland. When she felt Adam's arms wrap around her, he always made her feel safe. She longed for that feeling again, for the feeling of his skin on hers. The way his ribcage felt solid as it steadied her against him. She wanted to twist the fabric of his shirt between her fingers, until she could pull his shirt over his head and let her nails rake down his chest, leaving red trails of friction in their wake. She felt a pang in her stomach when she thought of her fingers tracing the tattoo on his ribcage, the one she could never seem to scratch off.

The first time she saw it was in her old bedroom, back in the house she grew up in. It was his first time back in her space since she broke up with him before prom. The boy she always loved stood before her, but he felt different somehow, as if her betrayal had changed something in his chemistry. As if the specter of her choice stood between them, the monster who masqueraded as freedom, who she chose over him. She would regret her decision every day for years to come. The marked boy stood before her with questioning eyes and open arms, with a black raven staring back at her from the ribs she knew so well. From beak to tail it took up nearly half of his ribcage. The black ink made him different, it made him brave. He never told her what it meant, but to her it was the ever-watching and silent reminder of the dark side of love. The side that waited quietly until its prey became vulnerable.

Sometimes when she looked at it, she felt a distinct emptiness, like the spaces between her fingers that were filled by the fingers of Doubt or Worry, who took her hand and led her into a dark place she mistook for freedom. The raven reminded her not to stray into the darkness again.

Then the thought crept out of her mind, slithering out like a scared creature. All she was left with was the tightness in her throat and the dull ache in her chest. She longed to penetrate her quiet space, the home she carried inside herself, because that was the place she carried Adam.

She breathed deep breaths into her lower abdomen, remembering her meditative practices. The air coursing through her body felt quenching, like drinking a cold glass of water on an empty stomach. She felt it wind through her body inch by inch. Slowly, she felt like herself again, strong and weak all at the same time. She allowed herself to be both. So she tucked the thoughts of Adam away, folding them carefully like fine linen, pushing them into a drawer that felt far too small.

"Deep breaths," she whispered to herself.

Elizabeth fell softly to her knees, sat in the middle of the path she had been following, and resolved not to move until she knew exactly where she was going. She longed for a break from the path and from her internal dialogue. As she sat gently breathing for a few minutes, observing her thoughts coming and going as she had done during many meditations past, she was suddenly struck by something that she could only believe to be divine inspiration. It was a line from one of Alice's letters, the one she received right after she spoke to the raven in the meadow courtyard: *There are woods that lie beyond this meadow courtyard, and in them you'll see things you've never seen before. Well, actually, you have—you created them yourself.*

Did I create all of this? Elizabeth challenged herself. In truth, she felt lost most of the time, and seemed to come upon most of her encounters by happenstance, with the notable exception of the scenes she tried to create in her mind, like the meadow courtyard and the second appearance of the Tweedles. Even those fell just short, the elusive dandelion seeds that floated through her fingers and just beyond her reach, the lightning bugs that lit up by your ear only to darken and reappear ten feet away.

Still sitting on the soft forest floor, she decided to try again. She had no vision in her mind to focus on, just the creeping feeling of finding Alice somewhere in the darkness.

"I have to think of a sign that will show me the way," she whispered.

As she sat, still breathing calmly, she envisioned in her mind's eye a giant red arrow, a physical manifestation of a compass that would show her the way to where Alice hid in waiting. She felt the elation and the relief of knowing the way, and the resolve of finding her way to Alice. With her eyes still closed she smiled as she felt those feelings, letting them overtake her as she imagined the big red arrow.

Elizabeth opened her eyes and saw a revision of her imagined creation before her. It was a sign, but it was not an arrow, nor was it any shade of red. Where her floating arrow had once been erected boldly in her mind now stood a wooden sign with scribbled writing etched across its surface. The sign had been attached carelessly to a stick and pushed into the soft ground in front of her. Elizabeth walked up to it and traced her fingers along the freshly painted black letters. The handwriting matched the script on Alice's letters. She pulled her blackened fingertips away from the sign. The paint was still wet.

The sign read:

THIS WAY TO THE MAD HATTER'S TEA PARTY

and included a scribbled picture of a hand whose index finger pointed straight to Elizabeth's right, in the fashion of an old circus sign.

"Not exactly the way I pictured it," Elizabeth said quietly, as she searched her surroundings for any trace of Alice. Her only company was her inner dialogue. She wondered how she could have let herself become so vulnerable in a strange place, sitting with her eyes closed as Alice read her thoughts and painted the sign in front of her while muffling a maniacal laugh. *If she put the paintbrush down and came closer she could've—*

Her trail of thought went instantly cold—not even her own thoughts felt safe anymore.

Her search for Alice had left her empty-handed again. With her mind momentarily void of thoughts, it became clear that the only direction she could go in was the direction the painted hand pointed her to. There was a path to her right, cut jaggedly through the grass as if with scissors, which she had not noticed before, if it had even been there before at all.

Elizabeth's thoughts suddenly grew darker, mirroring her surroundings. She was sure that she had not pictured Alice, yet Alice must have been standing near her, watching her while she sat with her eyes closed. She wondered if she was following Alice, or if Alice was following her, waiting for a moment of vulnerability to strike. But this was different. This was a game of cat and mouse played with someone who knows you more intimately than you know yourself.

Alice must be able to read my mind, like the Cheshire Cat, she reasoned. *Good. I'm glad. That way she knows I'm coming for her, and that I'm not leaving here without meeting her face to face.*

Elizabeth marched on toward the Mad Hatter and his tea party, though she was unsure of what she was marching into. She felt that what must lie beyond the path and the trees that lined it in chaotic, distressed lines was beyond anything she could possibly envision. She was ready to meet her next friend, or her next monster.

Instead, appearing after the gracious invitation that arose from her last thought of him, the Cheshire Cat materialized before her, standing on his head. It was not the absurdity of his stance that Elizabeth found to be his signature, but his cackling, demented laugh.

"I wouldn't go, if I were you," the Cat sang. Small twigs snaked out of his way as he bounced several times from his tail back to his head, and then landed on the mowed path beside her. When he got back on his feet, he contorted his body to make his legs appear slender and long in a provocative way, like a pinup girl. With his hands on his hips and his long legs accentuated, he mocked Elizabeth's walk in a way that exaggerated her sultry side. Elizabeth's own walk was more graceful, and with legs for miles, she always caught the attention of roaming eyes.

"Why are you walking like that? If you're trying to

mock me, that's not the way I walk," was all Elizabeth could respond. She was unsure if he was satirizing her, as she rarely had an accurate depiction of herself in her mind.

"You walk the walk!"

"And you talk the talk," Elizabeth fired back. She thought the Cheshire Cat only appeared at times when she already knew where she was going, just to bring attention to her own sanity.

"Insanity is genius, and genius is insanity!" he giggled, answering her thought. "A genius would go that-a-way." He stopped strutting and pointed back the way she came.

"And where would an insane person go?"

"Any way she chooses."

Like many of the paths in Wonderland, Elizabeth felt that this conversation was leading her in circles. "Why shouldn't I go to the Mad Hatter's? Have you been there before? If there's something I should know, you should say it now. Because as far as I'm concerned, that's where I'm going, genius or otherwise." She stopped in front of the Cheshire Cat and crossed her arms impatiently. The Cat grinned a toothy smile at her freshness.

"Do you remember," the Cheshire Cat mused, as he licked his paw and smoothed down one of his whiskers, "when you met a bird who called you a serpent?" he asked as his eyes flashed the kind of mysterious, dark wildness that made Elizabeth forget she was breathing for a moment.

"Yes, vaguely."

"You might just meet one yourself!" the Cat cried, with his disturbing gaze still fixed upon her. He then dissolved into a frenzied, staccato laughter that made her take a step backward. He appeared to be utterly, unquestionably insane.

"How right you are," he replied to her thoughts, though his voice echoed and trailed off as various parts of his body began to vanish. This time, it was his head that vanished first, followed by his twisted grin. After a few seconds, the only part of him left was his exaggerated, modelesque legs, distorted to the kind of perfection most only find in magazines, until they too disappeared.

"It's about time the prey starts playing games with the hunter," she said to the air where the Cat's sensuous legs once stood. She allowed her mind to dance with Doubt and Worry, who echoed the idea that the Cheshire Cat may have been right about the Mad Hatter, and that maybe she should turn around. But the thoughts were quickly eclipsed by the one reigning thought that had guided her this far: Find Alice.

Elizabeth began walking in the direction the sign pointed. Just as quickly as the Cat had vanished, a new scene took form as Elizabeth crested a small hill. Down in the valley she could see a table with matching chairs, which were almost indistinguishable from the forest floor beneath them, as moss, mushrooms, and small vines of ivy crept up their sides and covered almost every inch of their surface. It was as if nature had begun to reclaim the man-made, washing away the fake, sun-bleached ills of society. Next to the table stood a skinny tree with many branches but no leaves. It looked just like all the other trees in the forest, but this one stood out to Elizabeth because of the four silent ravens that were perched on its lower branches hanging just above the table, which was seated for five, though only one seat was occupied.

As odd as the scene was to Elizabeth, it was the fifth chair, the occupied one at the head of the table that drew her attention and would not let it go. Her eyes were held hostage by the sight of the Mad Hatter himself, but she did not seek release. As soon as she saw him, her body automatically came to a stop, as if she had to take in every inch of his appearance. The Mad Hatter's dark features were handsome in a nontraditional way that instantly disarmed her. Though she could not tell the color of his eyes from this distance, she suspected they matched the hazy bottom of an abyss that she longed to fall into, if only for a moment. The hue of a shaded lake you long to dip your toes into on sticky August nights. He sat relaxed against the back of his chair, which came up to just above his lower back. With one leg crossed over the other in a carefree way, he balanced one cup of tea in each palm, which were raised ear-level, as he casually rested his elbows on the mossy armrests of his seat. A third cup of tea was balanced on the top of his tall, black velvet hat.

Elizabeth continued her approach as if in a dream; her feet barely seemed to touch the ground. She floated toward him like a cloud, though he did not notice her until she stood just a few feet from the chair that was next to his. Finally, when his eyes met hers, she felt her walk slow and become more deliberate, and she remembered the Cheshire Cat's strut. When she reached the chair beside him, their eyes were still locked in a fierce battle of will as to who would break their gaze by speaking first.

She slid her fingers slowly across the top of the mossy chair.

"Come here often?" he asked. His voice was as smooth as butter, but the half grin on his face made her walls crumble, and for a moment she felt like she could finally vie for the spot of the hunter in this charade.

"What a horrible line!" Elizabeth retorted coyly, batting her eyelashes at him before lowering her gaze.

Suddenly, she remembered the lines under her eyes, and the way her makeup would crease and fall into them like quicksand, making them more obvious. The way her hair never fell over her shoulders the right way, and the way her shoulders slumped when she wasn't paying attention.

Then Adam's face flashed across her mind, and her heart rate quickened.

"Don't be shy, have a cup of tea," he said, as he put down the teacups he was holding and pulled out the mossy chair next to his, his third cup still balancing on his top hat. He moved with such grace and deliberate action that not a single drop spilled. Then he reached across the table and lifted a white teapot etched with pink trim, a pattern Elizabeth recognized, and poured tea into a cup in front of her that had an overgrown mushroom for a handle.

"Thanks," she said.

"So if you don't come here often," the Hatter asked, his eyes still lingering on her as he traced the rim of the teacup in front of him with his index finger, "then why are you here?"

"I was invited, actually. Although I was led to believe that there was going to be a party, but now that I'm here I see that it's just—"

"Just you and I," the Hatter interrupted, still smiling softly.

There was a slight pause that made Elizabeth uncomfortable, though she wasn't sure why.

"So, are you going to ask me a riddle about a raven or something?" Elizabeth said to break the silence, and the ravens on the branches near the table bobbed their heads with delight but said nothing.

"Why would I do that? I don't know any, I'm afraid."

"I just expected something like that."

"Nothing here is like you would expect. I hope I haven't disappointed you." His dark features seemed soft to her, drawing her in. With her defenses down she swam in the light he was emitting from his black eyes.

"Of course not. The opposite, actually. I think you're the first normal person I've met here."

More silence, but this one seemed filled with invisible threads of possibilities. She wondered to herself if he could be the one to give her the answers she so desperately sought. She felt that she could confide in him, tell him everything, bear her soul, and wipe her hands clean of Doubt and Worry. He had yet to shed the half grin that splashed across his face from the moment he first saw her.

"How dreadful. I haven't introduced myself properly, then, because if I had you would have known that I'm far from normal."

"I know who you are. I'm—"

"I know who you are," he interrupted. He inched closer to her and spoke in a hushed tone so that she had to lean in to hear him. "You're not normal either. So let's stop pretending."

"Fine," she whispered back. "So you're the Mad Hatter?"

"I'm quite mad, yes."

"And you're wearing a velvet top hat."

"Then I must be him after all."

"So maybe I'm not normal either. What does 'normal' mean in Wonderland, anyway? So what makes you so unusual, aside from being mad?"

"I'm not afraid of death," he said with a smirk.

"That seems pretty mad to me."

"I die to myself every moment. In fact, death is the essential truth of our existence," he mused. He carefully picked up his two teacups and balanced one in each upturned palm again. "Everything we love vanishes."

"I guess that's true, but how can you live with that kind of impermanence?"

"The same way we all do," the Hatter said with confidence. Noticing that the teacup in his right palm was empty, he put it back on the table, and a new teacup suddenly materialized next to it. He then quickly replaced Elizabeth's teacup with the full cup that still sat on top of his hat and put the new teacup back on his palm, as if nothing unusual had happened. His eyes remained fixed on her the whole time.

Elizabeth bit her lip. The Hatter could not take his eyes off of her.

"So tell me about yourself," she asked. "What do you do here in Wonderland, have tea parties by yourself all day?"

"I know nothing about myself."

"Because you keep dying to yourself?" she said with a laugh, winding a strand of her long, black hair through her fingers.

"Exactly."

"I know that feeling. Just earlier today—"

"Have you ever experienced a thought disappearing?" he interrupted, still balancing the teacups in his palms.

"Sure, of course I have. I probably lose as many as a thousand thoughts before breakfast," she said, feeling like the Hatter's riddles may have finally just begun.

"Only a thousand? Pity. When our thoughts disappear, who else disappears?"

"We do?"

"You do. I do. Our sense of self is created by our thoughts, and by the habit of the grasping mind. It swings from thought to thought like a monkey on a vine."

Elizabeth studied his face for a moment. His black eyes flashed a warning look, and he almost spilled the teacup resting in his left palm. He suddenly seemed to react badly to the intimacy of her probing eyes, though his freely searched hers. Suddenly, she felt the presence of something sinister yet invisible in the chair next to her.

The Hatter's eyes were locked on her, and for reasons she couldn't comprehend, she fished the compact out of her back pocket. The mirror was her only weapon against the masked madness around her.

"But you have to know something about yourself," she said, faking a tone of sweetness, as she grasped the mirror. "If you sit all day by yourself, just you and your thoughts. When your thoughts evaporate like the steam of this tea, when you disappear, there must be something left of yourself that you know very intimately?"

"So it's intimacy you're after," he said. He set the teacup resting in his right hand down on the table and placed his hand on top of hers. Elizabeth felt a tingling sensation rush up her arm, making her arm hairs stand on end. It filled her with the same disturbed feeling she had after she read Alice's last note, the one she found in the wall of branches, which still rested in her back pocket with the others. She pulled her hand back and put it in her lap. Just like that, she became the hunted.

"Intimacy with myself, maybe. What are you after?" she asked, as she placed the compact flat on the table without opening it.

"Th-that's not necessary," stuttered the Hatter. "There's no need for that. I'm after something much rarer than any silly reflection."

"Yeah? And what's that?" she asked, her hand still resting on the compact.

"I'm after you."

She opened her mouth to speak, but her words caught in her throat. She felt them beat against her insides, groping for air.

"Well, I'm after someone else," she said, as the memory of Alice's blue dress winding around the corner of the marble labyrinth flowed through her mind again. "And I may be afraid of both her and of myself at times, but that's not going to stop me from looking. I'm not going to distract myself with others to avoid looking at myself."

"I think it's time for new tea!" the Mad Hatter boomed. His voice startled the ravens in the tree beside them.

As he poured the contents of the fresh pot of tea into her cup and his, she saw something peculiar about the steam that caught her eye, distracting her.

"If it's fear you're looking for, I have just what you need," he whispered into her ear. "In the steam of the teacup you'll see what you fear the most."

The heat of his breath on her neck made her stomach turn over, as she gazed into the steam climbing up over the rim, its effervescence dancing before her eyes like waltzing ghosts.

Slowly, shapes began to take form. She saw a mirror with Alice's reflection staring back at her, her wide blue eyes revealing an anarchic madness to match her twisted smile.

"This is insane!" Elizabeth yelled, as she pushed the teacup away, breathing heavily and gripping the table, feeling the soft moss crumble underneath her grasping fingertips.

"Or is it complete genius?" the Hatter cooed, placing his hand on her knee in consolation. "Why don't you tell me what you saw?"

She stared blankly ahead and pushed his hand away. His handsome face could no longer mask his madness, and Elizabeth no longer felt inclined to trust someone who knew nothing of his own inner workings. The abyss she had once seen in the Mad Hatter's eyes revealed itself to be nothing but empty space.

"Don't touch me!"

"Alice, calm down. I didn't mean to—"

"Alice?"

"Come on, Alice, I only—"

"My name's Elizabeth, and you need to get away from me, now!" she warned, grabbing her compact from the table and holding it in her clenched fist. "I can't imagine what you see when you look into your own teacup, but I'm guessing you saw nothing! Not because you're fearless, but because you only see the person right in front of you instead of looking within yourself!"

He reached out to touch her arm, but she pulled away.

"I see you for who you really are. You're a snake. A snake ruled by the temptation of becoming lost in another. I have no intention of being your next victim."

The Hatter gazed back at her with fierce eyes, and the ravens cocked their heads to look at her.

"Why would Alice invite me here? Did she think you could scare me off? Well, guess what! It wasn't your face that I saw in the steam of the teacup," Elizabeth hissed.

Suddenly, out of the corner of her eye she saw the steam from her teacup begin to dance once more. Before her eyes, the steam seemed to part and come together as if someone was tracing through it with an invisible pen, forming words in handwriting that made the hairs on the back of her neck stand at attention. After several seconds, as the world around her stood frozen, Alice's next letter came to life.

Thanks for proving me right, little girl. You're scared of what you see in the mirror! And who was it you saw in the mirror just now?

I wonder how Adam would feel if he saw old Hatter's slimy hands all over you. That's right, I saw the whole thing. You were too busy looking into his black, reptilian eyes to see that there may have been one more guest at the table. I guess it can be our little secret.

But there's something you should know about secrets, sweetie. The only way two people can keep a secret is if one of them is dead.

The Hatter was right about death, though, as crazy as he is. (And you thought he was normal, are you that desperate?) When our thoughts disappear, we die along with them. But it's not time for you to leave Wonderland yet. What are you waiting for? Come and get me, if you think you can. Unless you prefer the company of snakes.

You know how to find me. Follow me into the darkness. I'll be waiting for you, slut.

— Alice

Elizabeth reached out to touch Alice's horrific masterpiece, but her finger moved straight through the steam as it dissolved before her eyes. Her gaze then darted quickly to the Hatter, who was still staring at her, licking his lips.

"I'm not Alice," she said, as her voice shook. "You have no idea who I am, but I'll show you who you are!"

Elizabeth grabbed her compact and thrust it toward the Hatter, who jumped back, toppling his chair. The teacup that rested on his hat crashed to the floor, cracking into sharp slivers of white porcelain. Elizabeth pushed the mirror toward him.

"Take a look! Look at the snake!" she demanded, her voice growing so loud that the ravens flew off the branches. "Next time you want to invite a girl in, make sure you know who she's really talking to first!"

Elizabeth snapped the compact shut and stuffed it back into her pocket. Her green eyes flashed a parting look that told the Hatter she would not be bitten.

She ran. She ran so fast that the steepness of the hill hardly slowed her down. But even over her struggling breath, she could hear the Hatter's possessed screams echoing behind her.

"Alice!" he wailed like a wounded beast. "Please come back, Alice!"

His voice pierced Elizabeth's ears. He sounded more animal than human. As she ran up the hill, leaving his maddening shrieks behind, Elizabeth decided that he was neither. He, too, was a monster.

"Alice!" he boomed again, followed by a blood-curdling scream that made Elizabeth's heart pound. It didn't sound like he was following her, but merely meandering around the table, occasionally collapsing into despair.

"I'm not Alice," she panted with disgust as she neared the crest of the hill at last.

When Elizabeth reached the top of the hill, she too collapsed, but not in a frenzy like the Hatter down below. She laid flat on her back, her chest rising and falling angrily, like waves crashing on a shore in a storm. The only thing that kept her anchored to the ground beneath her was her breath, and her vow that she would find Alice, regardless of the darkness ahead. She thought of the ravens. She thought of Adam.

"Follow me into the darkness," she repeated, closing her eyes as she felt herself fall away. Adam's eyes were the last thing she saw.

Nine

Elizabeth opened her eyes after a few minutes, awakened by a sharp pain coming from her forehead. Her eyelids fluttered harshly at the light. As she made out the shapes around her, she leapt to her feet in shock. In place of Wonderland's meadows and forked trees, she saw a table with an overturned clock and a Buddha statue. From her pink yoga mat she caught a sweet scent coming from the kitchen and heard clanging pots and pans, as Adam shuffled about, right where she left him.

Next she heard Fitz's rumbling paws race across the old Persian carpet, followed by a streak of creamy white fur as he raced to her side.

"Fitz!" Adam called with a whistle from the kitchen. "Come back here, boy! Your mom is trying to meditate."

"Adam?" Elizabeth cried, as the word caught in her throat. "Are you there?"

"Where else would I be?" he called back to her, popping his head out from behind the kitchen cabinets.

She rubbed her eyes, adjusting to the light.

"*I dream of us together, a little dream I dream every night,*" she heard Adam sing from behind a kitchen cabinet. His voice floated toward her in perfect pitch despite the fact that she knew he hated to sing. *"Wondering if you dream of me too,"* Adam continued. *"Because for better or worse I think we might . . ."* he closed the cabinet shut.

"Since when do you sing?"

"Be together forever!"

"Adam?"

"Are you done with your meditation already? You just sat down a minute ago!"

"Yeah!" she laughed and shook her head. "I'm so happy to see you, you have no idea! I have so much to tell you!"

She picked Fitz up and held him close, cradling him in her arms and kissing his forehead before she put him back down at her feet.

"Really? Did you reach nirvana in less than sixty seconds? That's got to be a record."

Elizabeth felt like running to Adam, wrapping herself around him, and never letting him go. An invisible string that connected the two of them drew her to him, constantly pulling them back to each other. The string tightened as she skipped toward him. But then she felt the tug of a second string, this one coming from somewhere inside her, and it pulled her toward the medicine cabinet in the bathroom, where her black velvet pouch waited. She flashed him a smile as she raced past him, Fitz trailing behind her in his usual way. Instinctively, she hopped over the spot on the rug where Adam's light blue sneakers had been, though the spot was empty now.

"No, it's not that, I just—"

Her words were cut short, as she entered the bathroom and saw a blank wall above the sink, which glared back at her like a black hole.

"Just what?"

"What happened to the medicine cabinet in here?"

I am strong. I am strong and in control.

"The what?"

"The medicine cabinet, obviously!" she yelled back to him, as she began tearing the bathroom apart. She was looking for her perfume bottle in the hopes that it would lead her to the black pouch that usually hid behind it. Fitz sat by the door, watching her.

"I have no idea what you're talking about, my love, but come out here and tell me about your experience. I'm making you those cinnamon pancakes you love!"

Cinnamon pancakes? Elizabeth wondered as she carelessly pulled down two towels from the towel rack, which landed on top of the heap of toiletries she had tossed out from underneath the sink. *Did I tell him I liked cinnamon pancakes? He's never made them before.* Her hands began to shake, as she piled the extra toilet paper, old lotions, and Adam's shaving kit back under the sink. Her pills had disappeared, but her craving for the sweet pills that would mute the incessant thoughts in her head was far from gone.

"Sorry, coming!" Elizabeth called to him.

"What's up with you today? Here I am making you your favorite pancakes, like I do every morning, and you're in there tearing the bathroom apart!" Adam said as he put two plates stacked with pancakes on the table by the living room couch.

"Anyway, the suspense is killing me. Sit down and tell me about your wild one-minute meditation!"

Elizabeth watched him from a distance with narrowed eyes.

"Are you going to keep me waiting all day, silly?" he said.

"*Silly?* You never call me that."

"Of course I do! When you deserve it," he laughed.

She moved over to Adam and sat slowly down beside him. She took a fork to the pancake at the top of the stack. It was fluffy, warm, and perfectly made, despite the fact that in their years of living together he never made them before. They melted in her mouth.

"I have to say, I'm impressed."

"Thank you!" he said with a singsong voice as he leaned in to kiss her. "Thank you, thank you!"

This was one of the first times she had ever heard Adam say these words, or, at least, not without looking down at the floor and rubbing the back of his neck first. But this time his eyes remained fixed on her.

"So? Did you reach enlightenment in under five minutes?" he pressed.

"Not quite," Elizabeth continued, still leaving ample distance between them on the couch. "I don't know where to start or how to explain it, but I feel like I've been gone for so long. I wasn't here in our apartment. I was in Wonderland! Don't give me that look, Adam. Just hear me out. It may seem strange, but I fell down a rabbit hole, and the next thing I knew, I was in Wonderland. Not exactly the Wonderland from the story, but my own weird, personal version of it, and it was really dark." She put her plate back on the table, nearly toppling a picture frame. "I know this may sound crazy, but I swear it was the realest thing I've ever felt. It was like I was really there! And Alice was there, too, only she wasn't a sweet little girl. Honestly, she was kind of a—"

Adam's eyes widened. "Elizabeth, are you feeling alright? What are you talking about?"

Fitz's eyes were also fixed on Elizabeth, as he sat by her feet, panting. She couldn't recall hearing him run over to join them.

"*Elizabeth?*" she repeated as she turned to look at Adam, who still hadn't touched his plate on the table. "You've called me Ellie since high school."

He shrugged. His smile remained plastered on his face. His hair lay perfectly flat on both sides.

"Look, I know how it sounds," she pleaded. "But please, hear me out. I think that finally, after years of meditation, I finally got one step closer to finding out who I really am. I got to explore this world inside of me that I had no idea even existed. It wasn't exactly a nice world. It was twisted, and it was filled with animals and people that I've never met before but somehow felt like I knew. Don't look at me like that. I'm not making this up! It all started after I fell down this rabbit hole, and then there was this marble labyrinth with creepy hallways, and—"

"I don't want this to sound insensitive," he interrupted. "But this just doesn't sound like you at all. I don't know what happened to you this morning, but maybe you should talk to someone about these dark thoughts you're having."

"Talk to someone? I'm not crazy, Adam! You need to hear about some of the things I found. All of these letters from Alice—"

"Please, Elizabeth, take a breath and eat your breakfast. Do you need some water? Maybe you should lie down for a while. I'll call the studio and let them know you're taking a sick day."

She clenched her jaw. "Stop calling me Elizabeth, and stop interrupting me! If you'd let me finish, you'd know I'm not crazy! I don't know if any of it was actually real or not. But it almost doesn't matter, because I know it was real for me. It felt just as real as sitting here with you right now. I know I went there for a reason. There was a bigger purpose to it all. It's as if my whole life I was meant to find Wonderland."

Fitz cocked his head to the side.

"I had to find Alice, she was the one who was guiding me the entire time!"

"I didn't say the word 'crazy,' you did. And I'm not calling you that," Adam said. "I'm just concerned. You've been acting strange. Why don't you put your feet up and eat the rest of your pancakes, and then maybe—"

"I'm acting strange? Look at you! I come out of my meditation, and you're cooking me pancakes that you've never cooked before, even though you say you do it every morning, even though I'm pretty sure that I've never once in my life told you that I even like cinnamon pancakes . . . and your sneakers! I tripped over them this morning, and now I don't see them anywhere. And why is the medicine cabinet gone? Did you get rid of it during my meditation?"

"Elizabeth, please calm down," Adam said softly, as he

stood up and carried his plate back into the kitchen. "I have no idea what you're talking about. My sneakers are right where I always keep them, under the bed and out of the way. And you know I make these pancakes every morning, and that we don't have a medicine cabinet. Even if we did, you were only sitting in meditation for a minute, how would I have been able to go in there, take it down, and get it out of here without you noticing?"

Just then, Adam reemerged from the kitchen with a tray of freshly baked cookies. He put them next to her pancakes on the table, nearly pushing the photograph of the two of them at the beach off the table.

"Chocolate chip cookie?" Adam asked with a stare and a wide smile. "I know they're your favorite."

For the first time since she came out of her meditation, she took a good look into Adam's eyes. They were lifeless and black, like a doll's eyes. Any traces of his once brilliant green-flecked eyes were absent, replaced by two black voids.

Elizabeth jumped up and took several steps backward, nearly tripping over Fitz, who stared back at her with the same lifelessness in his black eyes, which seemed even darker than usual.

"What's wrong, Elizabeth?"

"Stop calling me that! You never call me Elizabeth. You never make breakfast. And you never bake cookies. Where is this coming from? And what's wrong with Fitz?"

Fitz barked at the sound of his name, but his eyes remained expressionless, as if buttons could replace them and convey the same emotion.

"By the way, before I forget," Adam said, as if he had not

seen her jump out of her seat. "It's your mother's birthday next week, so I arranged to send flowers. Roses, of course. I know they're her favorite!"

Shadows slipped into his black eyes, lapping up his pupils like dark waters. His words faded into the background, as she glanced around their apartment and noticed that things weren't as she remembered them to be before her meditation. It was still a studio apartment, and as far as she knew she was still in Brooklyn, but the stack of bills on the table was gone. The old, unread cooking magazines that her mother used to send her were no longer piled on the kitchen counter or by the door. The cracked paint around the door had been painted over. She glanced at the picture frames on the shelves above her meditation space, which were still there but noticeably dustless. There were also several additions, all of which were from their high school years. There was a picture of the two of them smiling and wearing sashes that read "Prom Court." There was another photograph of them at a restaurant near where they grew up in, which showed Adam kissing Elizabeth's cheek as she blew out a candle of the number seventeen on a cake, despite the fact that Adam had forgotten Elizabeth's birthday that year. There was also a picture of her sitting on a picnic table with Adam at his family barbeque, though she never went to one of his family's barbeques. It was before the raven tattoo.

And her pills were gone.

"Elizabeth?"

She took a step toward the table and picked up the framed photograph of them at the beach, her favorite picture of her and Adam. Two smiling faces peered back at her, but they were not faces she recognized. Like the voids currently staring back at her from Adam's face in the kitchen, and from Fitz's on the floor by her feet, both of their eyes were black as her Alice doll's, which had silently gone missing from the shelf.

Normally, whenever either of them stared at this photograph, reflecting on the path that led them to where they are now—often privately and spontaneously, spurred by a familiar song lyric, or a floating, rogue memory—the thoughts were sometimes accompanied by wet tracks of tears on their cheeks, paved by the love they felt for one another. Before fate brought them together at a high school dance, they had spent their lives trying to make islands of themselves. And then they realized that the truest form of courage was looking into the eyes of the other and, seeing themselves stripped of superficial conventions and societal decay, feeling a love so intense that each of their souls conceded private ownership. They belonged to one another, as if they were two halves of the same soul, folded into one another with a divine symmetry. But as she gazed at the photograph now, something felt different. She looked over at Adam, who stared at her from the kitchen with an artificial smile plastered across his face.

"This isn't my apartment," she said quietly. "This isn't real. This is . . . hell."

"What are you talking about?" Adam asked sweetly. "Is something wrong? Can I make you something? I'm not sure what you could possibly need. Everything is perfect here! Aren't you happy here, Elizabeth?"

"Stop calling me that!" she screamed. "You're right. This

place is perfect, but it's too perfect, and you're not the Adam I've been with for nine years! Where is my Adam? What is this place?" Her shrieks bounced off of the walls. "I don't know how I got here, but none of this is real!"

She hurled the photograph at the wall above her yoga mat with all of her strength. The frame slammed against the wall, but it was the wall that fractured like a broken mirror. A few shattered pieces fell to the floor. She didn't notice Adam's face, which still stared back at her with a blank expression from the kitchen, nor did she notice Fitz's glazed glare. She did notice that some paint had scraped off the wall upon impact, revealing something distinctively reflective beneath its surface.

She ran to the wall and began tearing at the cracks. The glass broke off and fell to the floor, shattering into more pieces. As she peeled the shards away, she saw that a layer of bare, cracked cement was hidden underneath. Her fingers bled as she tore the glass away from the cement, but she felt no pain as she ripped each sliver away. Fitz started barking, and she could feel a sting in the center of her forehead, as she was pulling the walls down around her. Her panting breath, which grew more labored by the second, drowned out the deafening sound of Fitz's barks and the shattering glass.

Finally, standing in a pile of painted glass, the bare, cracked wall stood before her, streaked with her blood. The trail of blackened droplets spilled over letters that were scratched onto the surface. It looked as if someone had dragged their fingernails down the cement in a hurry. The letters were twisted, frantically written in cursive. She ran toward Adam and turned her back to him, standing inches away from him, to get a better view of the sentences etched on the cement wall that read:

Why would you ever want to leave here? Are you crazy?

Everything is perfect here, and it's all yours. It's everything you've ever wanted! You can stay here . . . forever.

Or you can come and find me. I'm still waiting for you in the darkness.

—Alice

One drop of blood descended down the wall, sliding down the "A" in Alice and onto the floor. She turned around to face Adam, who smiled back at her as if nothing had happened.

"Adam, or whoever you are, I'm going back. I'm going back into my meditation and back to Wonderland," she said, though she was uncertain if she had truly left. "I can't live in a perfect world, especially one that isn't real."

Adam continued to stare at her with his cold, black eyes.

"But Elizabeth," he said, the same mechanical smile plastered across his face. "It can be real, if you believe it is! Isn't everything here exactly how you wanted it to be? Pretend with me, Elizabeth. Our life is perfect, the apartment is perfect, and we're perfect together. Why don't you stay?"

"That's exactly why I can't stay," she said, biting the inside of her lip. "The clutter, the unpaid bills, your sneakers, even the years we left out of our collection of photographs . . . those are the flaws that make my world real. Not this."

"But we could be happy here! Everyday I'll cook for you, and we can be nothing but in love. We can make our life together exactly the way we want to! We—"

"No, we can't. I can do that with the real Adam, when I make my way back to him," she said, as she gazed at his black eyes with a twinge of sadness. "And I could never live in a perfect world knowing that I could never look into his green eyes again. Even if we're not perfect, I need to feel him looking back at me."

Adam reached out to Elizabeth and put his hand on her crossed arms. She pushed his hand away, but didn't turn. Suddenly, she felt herself pulling him toward her, digging her fingers into his back and pressing her chest to his. He was cold, still, and steady. Her fingers found the hem of his shirt, which was stiffly pressed and smelled like bleach, and traced his ribcage for any quiet indentations that the trails of ink left behind. She wanted to feel feathers manifest between the lines of his ribs and to feel the raven's beak rise to meet her thumb. Her fingers met bone and smooth, icy skin. The cold on her fingertips left her feeling numb. He wasn't the marked boy. He wasn't her Adam.

She was sad not to find his tattoo on his ribcage, the permanent reminder of a dark time that flapped its wings into quiet moments, whispering to her that he wasn't the boy he used to be, that she had somehow caused the darkness lingering below his skin. But the darkness was a part of the man he had become, the man she loved. This Adam was untouched by her faults, unmarred by their shortcomings, breakups, and time apart. She wasn't sure if she would erase the real Adam's tattoo, and she wasn't sure if that made her happy or sad, or if it was possible to be both, or if that's what a perfect world was.

Her vision blurred and her eyes stung. She turned away from him to face the broken wall.

Fitz barked as she sank to her knees, wiped her eyes, and crawled a few feet to her yoga mat, which was covered in glass. The corner next to the table with the Buddha was mostly clear of debris, and she sat down to face the statue as she pulled her legs into her chest, letting her spine curve into itself. She took a breath. Then she reached out her right hand and laid it flat on the floor. She closed her eyes, took a few more breaths, and found herself surrounded by darkness once again.

Ten

Elizabeth opened her eyes and found herself on her back, staring at a dark, cloudless sky. It was nearly black and seemed infinitely deep. Sitting up on her elbows, she looked around her, struggling to catch her breath, taking in the familiar scene of Wonderland.

"I'm back," she panted, clenching the long meadow grasses in between her fingers. "Or I guess I never really left."

There was a dull ache in her chest where she felt Adam's absence. She knew that wanting him meant wanting Alice. She had to find the truth that Wonderland hid, so she could make her way back to him and to her life, as imperfect as it was. Her reality grew darker and darker, mirroring her surroundings. The shadows that were once strewn upon the forest floor were gone, as if they melted into nightfall. She looked up at the moonless Wonderland sky and let herself cry. She may have been afraid of the message Alice carved into the wall of her fake apartment, of seeing her blood streaked across the walls, of Alice's image she saw emerge in the steam from the teacups, but she wasn't afraid to cry.

Elizabeth let herself sink into her own abyss, giving birth to little thoughts with loud cries. She thought of the real

Adam and her old life, the one that may or may not still be unfolding in some parallel reality, where she might still be sitting in the lotus position meditating, surrounded by the two souls that loved her most.

She thought of Adam's forest green eyes and the beauty of his spirit. It was one of those moments when she was just thankful he existed and that their souls had come to meet in this one glorious life they shared together. He was her person. She knew he was the one she wanted to sit at the kitchen counter with on those long summer nights, talking into the early hours of the morning with a white ring forming around the corner of her lips and a half-empty glass of wine in her hand. He was the one she wanted to brush her teeth next to, and argue with over where the remote went. He was the one she wanted to make coffee for, even though he liked his black and she filled hers with chai, skim milk, and raw sugar.

She missed watching him from the bed, as he fumbled through his sock drawer while he got ready in the morning, rummaging for that elusive second sock in the pair, even though it was by his feet. She would point it out, and he would laugh the kind of laugh that made the wrinkles around his eyes come alive. He would push the hair out of his eyes, joking that she hadn't done the laundry in weeks, and she would shoot back that it would take him an entire day to figure out what all the knobs and settings on the washing machine meant. She thought one day she would look at him during one of those mornings, with her black hair tied up in a messy bun and her slippers dangling from her feet off the side of the bed, and see the crevices that were beginning to form around his mouth, and that his hair was turning gray, and that hers was too. She thought maybe he would look more like his dad, but with that charm that was all his own, dog fur still clinging to his boxer shorts. She smiled a little at how she would remind him that the lint roller was on the top shelf in the closet, but he still wouldn't find it. He would tell her he loved her before he walked out the door on his way to work.

She thought about conversations they had and conversations yet to be had, both the ones she would remember and the ones she would forget. The ones about bills, and the ones about vacations they wanted to go on but never took. The adventures they wanted to have, and the adventures they had—the time they got lost hiking, the time they tried to host a dinner party together but left the main course in the oven a few minutes too long, the time they painted the bathroom, and the time they got snowed in and went through all of their old family photo albums. She thought that one day, as she would flip through the glossy pages with "1995" written in faded ink on the sides, she would make a comment about her father getting older. Then she would regret being the dramatic one in the conversation, and he would remind her that her dad still had plenty of good years ahead of him, despite his back problems.

She thought about the kids they might have, the school plays they would sit through. Their little girl would say her one line, and Elizabeth would pretend she wasn't crying and then look over at Adam to see if he was. She thought about the parent-teacher meetings with the flat soda and stale butter cookies. The report cards that sometimes would be good and sometimes would be awful, and how they would debate like grand politicians the best ways to motivate the girl, but then remind one another that at least she's great at art and knows how to play two songs on the piano by heart. She thought about their future trips to theme parks, and about Adam complaining about the heat while misting himself with a plastic spray fan shaped like a princess, while the little one would tug at her pant leg.

He was the one she wanted to grow old with. The one she would let make fun of her as she tried on her first pair of reading glasses. The one who would accidently buy a matching pair for himself, because he forgot what hers looked like, and who would threaten to return them but never would. He was the one she wanted to squint at dinner menus with, the one she was excited to be old with, so they could complain about the process together, while filling out a morning crossword puzzle in the Sunday paper. He was the one she saw sitting next to her as they wrapped Christmas presents for their grandkids at one o'clock in the morning, with two empty wine glasses with a silhouette of Santa stamped on the front resting on top of the table covered in wrapping paper scraps and ninety-nine-cent bows. He was the one she wanted to fight with, the one she wanted to love forever, and the one she wanted the years to fly by with.

He was the one whose sneakers she wanted to trip over.

And when their beautiful life together was over, when the sands in the hourglass of their time together ran to nothing, he was the one she would want to say goodbye to.

Between her tears, she hoped for a moment that she could

blink and see her and Adam's apartment materialize around her, the real apartment with the clock still face down on their desk, just as she had left it.

Instead, she opened her eyes to the dark forest closing in on her, and the wild, beastly grin of the Cheshire Cat.

"Oh my God!" Elizabeth yelled as she sat up and crawled several feet back on her hands, which showed no signs of having been torn up by the glass walls of her fake apartment.

"Not God, just me!" laughed the Cat, with only his head visible in the twilight of their surroundings.

"For heaven's sake," Elizabeth panted. "You scared the hell out of me!"

"I know nothing of either place," the Cheshire Cat said, as he twisted his whiskers around one very sharp claw.

She wiped her tears away on the back of her hand, the thick and hot tears that lovers and saints shed, as she stood up. "I still feel totally lost here," she said with a cracked voice. "One minute I'm back in my apartment, and the entire apartment, and Adam and Fitz, aren't real. Even here, it's like everything is constantly changing! First, I meet someone here that I think is finally sane, and then they turn out to be just as crazy as everyone else . . . and now I'm here crying and talking to an orange head. I don't even know if this is the right Wonderland to fall back into from meditation. How do I know if I'm supposed to be here?"

"Of course you're supposed to be here!"

"Why?"

"Because this is the place you're in right now."

Elizabeth dropped her head in frustration. *If the most*

intelligent advice I'm getting is from a maniacal cat without a body,
I must be in deep. I must really be in trouble.

"Not in trouble, in luck!" the Cat said between psychotic
bouts of laughter. "What better way to find your courage
than to look in the deepest, most maddening crevices of the
mind!"

"Courage? I miss Adam, and I have a madwoman waiting for me who is always two steps ahead of me. She's been
leaving me breadcrumbs of insanity that have led me nowhere
this whole time. All this, so I can find out the reason I'm here.
Courage doesn't even begin to cover what I need."

"Now that's nonsense," the Cat said, as his head began to
slowly spin in circles. "You made the commitment to explore
the darkest realms of yourself when you sat down to meditate. You set that intention, didn't you? That promise brought
you here, and you set another intention to find Alice. You've
peeled away the layers of your mind one by one, putting your
most horrifying nightmares in your face to try to scare you
off your path. Believe me when I say that revelations work in
detail. In the face of these impossible obstacles, you're sitting
here crying! I say we celebrate!"

"*Celebrate?*" Elizabeth said, as she held her head in her
hands.

"Yes! When you dream of the impossible, my dear, it
doesn't come to fight you. It comes to help you fight back!"

"What? Have you lost any shred of sanity that you might've
had left?"

"I hope so! But now isn't the time to search for sanity.
Now is the time to dance our shamanic dance in the abyss

of the mind. By hurtling yourself into it, instead of lying in the grass questioning the process, you might discover that you are, in fact, lying on a feather bed."

Elizabeth stared at the Cheshire Cat. She thought he must either be the smartest creature she had ever met, or the most insane. Or both. But for a moment, the forest of Wonderland didn't seem so dark.

"Do you remember what I told you about silence?" the Cheshire Cat continued, as his head began to spin at the same rate in the other direction.

"I think so," Elizabeth recalled, thinking back to when they first met. *"You find silence only in the absence of your mind, where there is Nothing. Not even You.* Right?"

The Cheshire Cat didn't answer, but simply displayed his fangs in such a way that made him look like he was attempting to give his widest grin yet.

"Right," Elizabeth said, her voice trailing off with the remembrance of the fact that she was speaking to a dismembered head. "I'll keep going then." She wanted to add that she had to keep going without pills, that she had to find inner silence without them.

"And don't forget to smile!"

"If only I knew where to go."

"Did you not listen to anything I said?" the Cat hissed as the fur on his face stood on end. "You create the way! The path and the destination are both what you decide them to be."

She let his words sink in for a moment. Her conviction to return to her life with Adam and Fitz was outgrowing her conviction to avoid looking at herself in the mirror, and her fear of Alice. Her first experience in Wonderland, the caucus of animals at the base of the inverted, or non-inverted, bare oak tree, had taught her that escaping the surface layer of thoughts was necessary to move in either direction. She thought about her conversation with the butterfly and how it only led her in circles.

"Maybe you should have taken the orange pill after all!" boomed the Cheshire Cat, whose words were followed by more hysterics and staccato tones that rose and fell like her chest did just a minute ago. It was like the chanting of a madman.

"Stop laughing at me! I'm trying to think!"

The Cheshire Cat wiped his paw across his face as if rubbing off his smile.

Still following her trail of thought, she ignored the Cat's musing and continued to pace around his floating head. She calculated that she had passed through the superficial realm after meeting the Tweedle twins. They were distracted by their own looks and emphasized physicality over inner identity, which Elizabeth saw as ever-changing in itself.

"This may seem crazy, but, internally, it's just like a face or an eye," she wondered aloud. "The expressions are constantly changing, but the face within knows itself."

"Do you?" the Cheshire Cat asked, as the orange pattern in between his eyes furrowed.

She continued to run with her thoughts, as if she had not heard his question. She thought about Tweedle Dum and Tweedle Dee, and how they almost got their voice, but were so resistant to it that they almost turned violent.

"A mind for a mind makes the whole world thoughtless!" sang the Cat.

"And then the Mad Hatter, he was too busy charming his inner snake to look within himself."

"How awful it must be to wander the earth in thirst, looking for others to satisfy a lust for the self," mused the Cheshire Cat, as his dismembered head began to bob and weave around Elizabeth's body. "But snakes can shed their skin, you know. I've seen it happen."

Suddenly, the momentum of her reflection was cut short by the intrusion of the image of Alice's face in the mirror, her smile flickering in the steam of the teacup. The memory made Elizabeth's heart race, and the abruptness of her spiking pulse startled the Cheshire Cat, whose head hung upside down for a few moments before he could correct himself.

"Don't take this the wrong way, but I think you were right earlier. You are lost!" mocked the Cheshire Cat, whose orange fur changed from orange to yellow, to green, and finally to a dark violet that nearly camouflaged him in the darkness of their surroundings. "But you should take it as a compliment. The best people are."

"Sorry, I didn't mean to catch you off guard. It's just that sometimes, when I think of Alice, I guess I get a little crazy, just kind of confused," Elizabeth said. "It's like I know her. I can't explain it. Maybe it's beyond words. But there's something about her that feels familiar. Once I find out what that is, and why, I think I can come out of my meditation. I think that's when I can leave Wonderland."

At that thought, both Elizabeth and the Cheshire Cat

smiled, though Elizabeth's glow hardly reflected the spark of madness that colored the Cat's grin.

"Home!" Elizabeth said, as she closed her eyes and sighed with relief. Saying the word aloud gave her a boost of energy, as if it ricocheted within the inner chambers of her heart and made it beat faster and faster, like the beat of a drum that marched her onward into the darkness.

"So what's left, then?" the Cat asked excitedly. "Now that you've made it past the Mad Hatter and through the demented labyrinth of the mind?"

"All that's left to find is Alice. And myself. But really, I only have to find myself, because wherever I am, I'm sure she'll be."

For the first time since she met the Cheshire Cat, she saw him look confused. He looked at her as if she had lost her mind.

"Why are you looking at me like that?"

"If you want to find Alice, why don't you just go to her house?"

"Her *what*?"

"Alice's house! Where she lives, of course! It's just over there, beyond those trees. There's a small gate with a lock, and that's how you get to her house," the Cheshire Cat said casually.

"If you knew I was looking for Alice, why didn't you tell me that from the start?" Elizabeth asked with clenched fists.

"Because you got here yourself, didn't you? This is where you were heading all along, whether you knew it or not. Sometimes we only find what it is we're really looking for if we don't know what we're looking for!"

I wasn't looking for Wonderland, but I found that easily enough, she thought to herself, as she rolled her eyes.

"It's not about finding Wonderland," the Cat said with a grin like the crescent moon. "It's about finding yourself."

She relaxed her grip and bit her bottom lip. Not only had she found a direction, but she found the heart of Wonderland, right on Alice's doorstep.

"No offense, Cheshire," she said, as she smoothed out her shirt. "But I can't waste another second talking with you. I have to get back to Adam. I have to get back to my life!"

"Of course," he said, as his crescent moon smile grew wider and his eyes flashed with darkness. "I should only hope you find the key." After he uttered his last words, his face began to vanish, only his fangs lingered for a moment. They danced in front of her like two dueling ghosts and then disappeared, leaving her with her own silence.

"Whatever that means," Elizabeth said, as she rolled her eyes. Nonsense was becoming a second language for her.

After the image of the Cheshire Cat's phantom teeth left her mind, she left the meadow, moving toward the dark ridge of trees before her as if drawn by an enchanting flame. Once she reached it, she wound her way through several rows of forked trees and felt her way through the branches. Because of the growing darkness, it was more difficult than before. The bark under her fingertips was rough and cracked, and it stood in stark contrast to the feeling of the wrought iron gate, which she finally found after several minutes of wading through more branches and tree trunks. Like the original gate to the Wonderland forest, this gate was dark and twisted. But instead of a large, barred gate, there was a door in the middle of the thick bars, with a large keyhole in the center of it. Despite its dark and sinister appearance, Elizabeth could not help but notice the beauty in its vintage Victorian style and the ornate spirals that bordered the broad keyhole.

She studied the keyhole and wondered where she would find a key large enough to fit in the keyhole that was the size of her hand. Suddenly, she understood the Cheshire Cat's last warning.

She pushed on the door with all her strength but it wouldn't budge. She shoved the bars at its side, which seemed to stretch infinitely in both directions, and it didn't give an inch, or even let out a creak. After trying for several minutes to force her way in, Elizabeth crouched down to stare at the keyhole. A faint light emanated from its rusted metal outline, drawing her in. Slowly, she knelt down and put her eye to the broad keyhole, which was nearly half the size of her face, and glimpsed at what lay just beyond her reach.

She could barely make shapes out of the darkness, but through the keyhole she saw wild flowerbeds with brilliant red, yellow, and orange hues surrounded by walls of dark thorn bushes that replaced the spires of the black trees she had become accustomed to seeing as the background of this place. The walls of thorns created a labyrinth around the flowers, which licked the land like flames.

How do I find a key?

If she learned anything from her journey in Wonderland, it's that if there's a lock there's always a key, somewhere or other, even if it can only be found in her mind, which already felt sharper without Doubt and Worry. She thought that if she wanted to get through the door, she would have to find her breath, just as she had with the last door she came across.

She closed her eyes and began to concentrate on each breath. She was fully present for each inhale and exhale. With each breath she felt lighter, as if she could float over the door as the Cheshire Cat had floated through the air around her moments ago. To her own amusement, she imagined herself doing just that. She pictured herself becoming weightless, bouncing around in thin air as easily as the Cheshire Cat, bobbing and weaving like a dandelion seed caught in the wind. She pictured herself floating through the bars of the wrought iron fence, dancing around them as if she were playing ring around the rosy like she had as a child. Finally, she imagined herself shrinking to the size of a dandelion seed, carried by the wind, gliding gently through the large keyhole and landing on the other side, coming to rest at the foot of one of the walls of thorns.

As Elizabeth opened her eyes, she smiled to herself at the realization that for once she had gotten a visualization right. She stood exactly where she had pictured herself to be. She stood firmly and faced the wall of thorns that stared back at her, the ones that guarded Alice's secrets. Finally Elizabeth stood in Alice's garden, the one that the Cheshire Cat said would lead her to Alice's doorstep. The melancholy Wonderland forest drowned in darkness behind her.

Eleven

Alice's garden was blanketed in darkness and contained peculiar adornments the likes of which Elizabeth had never seen before. Since she could now see more of the scene than the keyhole's narrow view had allowed, she was uncertain as to whether or not she wanted to see the whole picture. She took a deep breath and began to make her way through the flowers and thorns. The walls of thorn bushes cast dark shadows on the ground that looked like bony fingers grabbing at her.

In Alice's garden, where the wildflowers grew at their own will, terrible and wonderful things lurked in the darkness that took hold of Elizabeth's senses. She felt a dark energy seep through every pore of her body, as she surveyed her surroundings. Lying strewn across the grass were small porcelain rabbits with cracked white paint. Some sat upright and some had been knocked over as if they had just been run through. Their chipped paint made them look fragile, as if some of their insides were showing. Each rabbit had a pair of painted red eyes that never blinked, which stared back at Elizabeth and made her shiver each time she caught their gaze. These were far from the white rabbits she had originally expected to find in Wonderland, but she came to learn that Wonderland was the home of both infinite darkness and light, even if the only light she could see was her own internal flame.

Next, she saw floating watering cans, which watered the flowers and thorn bushes mechanically, floating up and down, as if there were invisible strings attached to their handles. Their silver bodies hovered and glinted in the fading light, like mechanical butterflies floating above the flowers.

Through the garden there was a light breeze, which she couldn't feel on her skin but noticed by the movement of the flowers. She hoped it was a breeze, and not the plants moving by their own conviction. When the flowers moved together, a brilliant scale of reds, yellows, and oranges danced together, and the whole garden looked like it was on fire.

The garden made her think about what might await her in Alice's house. When she felt her heart begin to race, she grabbed at each breath as if it were a life raft. With each step, she reminded herself to breathe.

Breathe and get the hell out of here!

She quickened her pace as she gazed at the red, yellow, and orange beds of flowers that stretched out before her like a wildfire. But her mind far outpaced her walk as the sharp image of a sunflower, the same one that Adam brought for her on their first date, gripped her mind. She loved the way the bright yellow petals on the outside concealed the black center enclosed within. The image was followed by the recollection of a phrase, one that Elizabeth told Adam when they first started dating in high school: *You can tell a lot about a girl by the flowers she likes.*

"If that's the case with Alice, she really must be out of her mind," she said, and the small smile that crept across her face at the memory melted into the blackness of the night. She crept around the walls of thorns carefully, despite her quick pace, trying not to get so close that they would scratch her skin or tear her clothes. In some places, the path was very wide, as if someone had planted the bushes that lined it by haphazardly throwing seeds around rather than following lines of symmetry. She was careful to step over the porcelain rabbits, some of which were cracked into pieces, their skulls smashed, littering white fragments throughout the dark grass like stars engulfed in the black night sky. As she wound deeper and deeper along the garden's path, she saw other garden decorations, but they were far from the type she expected to find in a traditional garden. In place of hot pink flamingos were black ones. Distinctly painted on their black plastic backs were the bones forming a tucked wing, dots of neck bones, and a white skull attached to a bony beak. It was as if they were not flamingos at all, but cadavers who had been dissected and turned inside out. They looked liked walking skeletons in the darkness.

She thought to herself that Wonderland's darkness had a way of drawing the insides out.

"And what kind of person decorates their garden with—"

Her thoughts were cut short as she came upon a large sign, like the one pointing her in the direction of the Mad Hatter's Tea Party, with large cursive letters. This time the paint was dry, so dry that it cracked in several places, as if it had been standing in this spot for years. Against black painted wood the white letters read:

BEWARE THE STRAIGHT PATH. I MEAN, HELL, BEWARE OF ANY PATH. IF YOU FIND YOURSELF ON A PATH, GET OFF OF IT!

The letters were painted in all different sizes, as if Alice was slipping out of sanity with each stroke of her brush.

The image of Alice's smile in the steam of the Mad Hatter's teacup bubbled up in her mind. The same smile that seemed to follow her wherever she went. It was both in front of her and behind her, with every step of her journey.

But not for long, Elizabeth promised herself, as she stopped to take in the rest of the scene.

Littered around the base of the sign were several rabbit masks. They were white with red eyes, like the shattered replicas lying by her feet in the uneven grass. The sign was shoved crookedly into the ground, like a stake into the heart of a monster. Her eyes held on to each one for several seconds, soaking in the madness emitting from each pair of red eyes that stared back at her. Mingling with the masks were several scattered rhinestone tiaras, some of which were missing a few stones. Some were bent, as if they had been violently twisted and knotted in a fit of rage. Adding to the pile of horrors were several makeup brushes and a few lipsticks, some uncapped and exposing the red and pink pigment within, like they had bled to death. There were several uncapped mascaras, which looked like rusty daggers glinting in Wonderland's faded light.

"Are all of these mine?" Elizabeth asked, as she touched the makeup and shards of rhinestones cautiously with her foot, as if she were nudging a dead creature to see if it were still alive. "Well, these definitely aren't mine," she said as she nearly stepped on a rabbit mask. *These have Alice written all over them.*

No sooner had she thought the words when she felt something crunch beneath her leather boots. The object was black, and in the darkness she hadn't seen it lying in the blackness of her shadow. As she stepped backward, she saw a black velvet hat pop back into shape, coming back to life after she crushed it.

She covered her mouth with her hands to stifle a gasp and looked over her shoulder. To her relief—or silent despair—she discovered that she was alone, except for the company of the shattered rabbits, bird skeletons, masks, flowers, and thorns.

"There's no way he could have made it here and left it without me noticing," she reasoned to herself. *Unless he had help.*

If this was Alice's playground, then Elizabeth was sure she was not lost in a deep meditation, but facing the black straitjackets of her darkest nightmares, standing before them in thick mascara armor backed by an army of relentless thoughts.

Maybe I really did fall asleep. Everything here feels so real and so unreal, like a lucid dream, she thought. But every time she connected with her breath, she felt the invisible string that pulled her back to Adam and Fitz, to their apartment where she sat on her pink yoga mat. For a moment, she wondered if she could fly into Wonderland's black sky, with her arms out above her head, if she could touch that hand that rested on the wooden floor in Brooklyn, the hand that steadied her as she meditated. She looked up at the black dome of endless sky above her and saw only darkness. *Maybe I'm trapped in a lucid nightmare,* she thought, still gazing above, and she wondered if the sky really was a sky or just a reflection of herself, dark and infinite. Her eyes dropped back down to her feet, the dark grass, and the reality she knew she couldn't escape.

Suddenly, her train of thought was interrupted, as she caught sight of a shadow lying just behind the thick post of the wooden sign, its dull pale color barely glinting in the night. A few feet before Elizabeth, tangled in the wild, unkempt grass of Alice's garden, lie a mask of her own face, with its eyes cut out.

Her bright green eyes had been cut into long, black slits, so that its wearer could see through them. The nose, red lips, and full cheekbones were undeniably her own. She couldn't look away, and as she stood dead in her tracks with shaking hands and shallow breaths, she knew in that moment that this was far worse than any lucid nightmare she could have ever imagined. Her muscles began to contract all at once, as if some intuition residing deep within her told her to run, to scream, or to call out for help. Yet she stood frozen, looking at her own empty, black gaping holes for eyes that stared back at her.

"Who would do this?" she whispered, lacking the air and the courage to speak any louder. She tried to blink, hoping that somehow it would disappear. Then she thought to herself that she knew exactly who did this, and as Alice's name danced on her lips, she saw Alice's psychotic, twisted smile flash before her in her mind again. The mask, she thought, as sick and sinister looking as it was, could only have one owner deranged enough to wear it.

Suddenly, she felt overcome by a force that willed her to walk toward the mask. She lifted it and cradled it in her hands mechanically, as if she were a marionette and someone, somewhere was pulling her strings like the floating watering cans in the flower garden around her. As she held the mask of her own face in her hands, she ran her fingertips over its cold porcelain surface. It seemed so fragile, yet the empty black gaze emitting from the eyeholes of the mask aroused a certain strength in Elizabeth.

Everyone wears a mask here, and you do too, gorgeous, even if you don't think so. The words from Alice's first letter arose in her mind like a clearing in the thick fog.

"What if she's been right this whole time?" she whispered. She asked herself if she would know if she had been wearing a mask all along, and if that's something you could know about yourself or not. She wondered if Adam had known all along and if that's what he had tried to tell her before her meditation. She wondered if she was transparent, obvious to Adam and Alice, and oblivious to herself.

Elizabeth lost her grip on the mask. It fell out of her hands, as she stared blankly forward, lost in her revelation. It crashed at her feet into a million shards of white porcelain. The sound of the crash echoed against the wall of thorns on all sides of her, amplifying the sound back at her, drowning out the last few words of her thoughts.

"I'm finding Alice, and I'm getting out of here!" she said to the black wall of thorns around her. She longed to find Alice's house before the darkness could swallow her whole.

Yet, her pace was less confident. She walked faster and faster, as if she were trying to escape her own death. Then, just as she did through the marble labyrinth and around the dark corners of the Wonderland forest, Elizabeth found herself running, gaining pace with every stride, trying to outrun the shadows that were closing in on her. Gone from her mind was the hope that Alice could still become a benevolent guide, a savior who could release her from this place and guide her out of her meditation. The image she desperately clung to, as she chased her through the shadowy corridors at the bottom of the rabbit hole, had completely vanished.

I thought this was supposed to be my world. All I see around me is Alice's playground! My own personal hell.

They don't serve cookies in hell.

The line from Alice's first note ricocheted off of the walls of Elizabeth's mind as she ran through the dark, twisting pathways of the garden, with the flame-like flowers closing in on her from all sides.

She wondered if that was what Alice had tried to tell her from the beginning, that there was a hell on earth, and that it's called her subconscious. As her thoughts raced, she jumped over porcelain rabbits and dodged the uneven thorn bushes that stood in her way. She thought that if hell could become reality, a place that you could visit, the gates were Alice's front doorstep. If Wonderland was truly the white underbelly of her subconscious, she wasn't sure if she was ready to turn it on its stomach and look the beast in the eye.

"Ouch!" Elizabeth gasped when a large thorn cut her shoulder, as she tried to avoid running over a shard of white porcelain. She covered her shoulder with her hand and felt hot, sticky blood seep between her fingers. The pain forced her to slow down momentarily, but she marched forward to the beating of an internal drum. "Alice, ready or not, here I come."

"That doesn't make sense at all! Are you ready, or are you not?"

Suddenly, the fiendish laughter of the Cheshire Cat joined the echo of the cracking shards of broken rabbits. He floated behind her, just above her left shoulder, and wore one of the white rabbits' masks. She swung around to face him and jumped backward at the sight of the rabbit head bobbing on top of his cat body. His orange tail flicked back and forth with delight.

"So, how do I look?" he said, as the mask tilted off-center. She could tell that behind the mask he still grinned his satanic, wide grin, widening into a triangle that framed his pink, sandpaper tongue.

"Do you have to appear out of nowhere like that?" she asked, still holding her shoulder. "You scared me half to death!"

"Come on. I can't be worse than anything else in this garden! If you were scared half to death before, then I must be staring at a ghost."

"Look, I'm just trying to get to Alice's house and get out of here before it gets any darker."

"It's midnight in Wonderland," he said, raising his arms to the sky. "But don't fret, it always gets darker just before the dawn."

He began to bob up and down as he floated. The mask made him list even deeper from side to side, as it was nearly twice the size of his own head.

"Could you take that thing off? It's really starting to freak me out," Elizabeth begged, as she looked around her again, clenching her shoulder as the pain began to subside.

"Of course! All you had to do was ask," he said, as the mask disappeared from his face, taking his whole head with it. His body floated headless for a few moments, and his orange fur stood on his skin like the thorns on the walls around her. After a few seconds his head slowly reappeared, and he shook it as if he had just woken up from a long slumber.

"What was all that back there? The tiaras, the makeup, the masks. I don't understand."

"What do you mean? You know what they are!"

"Yeah, but I'm not sure—"

"Honestly, you're completely mad. You put them there. They're yours, of course!"

Elizabeth felt the space between her eyebrows begin to ache again. "What? I mean sure, maybe the makeup looked like mine, but I didn't put it there! And that creepy mask? That's something Alice would wear, not me. I'm not wearing a mask!" she cried, covering her forehead with her palms in frustration.

"That's the mask," he cooed.

As the Cat's words began to sink in, she squeezed her shoulder harder, and the sting of pain from her wound shook her out of her stupor. She instinctively rubbed her hands together, expecting the dried blood to flake off of her fingers like snowflakes, but her hands were clean. There was no sign of a scratch. The pain had been created and existed only within the confines of her mind. With that realization, she thought of her own ignorance as her morning flashed back in her mind: the makeup application, the way she avoided the mirror, the way she wore her own self-righteous crown as she argued with Adam.

"There! Now it's gone. Just be careful not to lose your head, too," the Cat warned.

"There's still one more thing."

"I'm listening," the Cheshire Cat assured her, though he was playing jump rope with his tail.

"In a letter I found from Alice she told me that I created this place, and that all of it comes from me," she said loud enough for him to hear her over his jumping. "But I don't feel like this place is my own at all. So maybe the makeup was mine, but what's with these rabbits? The phantom watering cans? The bird skeletons? I don't think I could make any of this up if I tried."

"Then you're more mad than I thought!" The Cheshire Cat choked out his words between fits of laughter, as if she had just told him a joke. "It's as if you wouldn't know your own house, even if you were standing in it!"

"My house? No, I'm trying to find Alice's house," Elizabeth sighed, wondering if he truly was crazy.

The Cheshire Cat jumped too soon and nearly lost his balance, as he tripped over his own tail. "It's not nice to call someone crazy, you know," he said, as he brushed himself off. "It's dismissive."

"Well it's not nice to listen to someone else's thoughts, either!" Elizabeth said with crossed arms. "And you just called me crazy!"

"No, you misunderstood me," the Cat said with a smile,

his white fangs standing out against the darkness. "I never said you were crazy, I called you mad! Two completely different things, my dear. Obviously."

"You're trying to avoid the question," Elizabeth said with narrowed eyes.

"What question?" the Cat asked, as he took his tail in his hands and began to tie the end into a bow.

"You said I wouldn't know my own house even if I were standing in it, like there was no distinction between Alice's house and mine. Why did you say that Alice's house was my house?"

He purred as he untied the bow, only to tie it again. "There's something you should remember about houses," he said, as he continued to fidget with his tail. "Even within our own house, there may be a room that we don't visit often, usually by choice. Maybe it's too dark, or maybe it doesn't feel like ours. Then, eventually, the place ceases to exist in our world. Or, we think it does. But the forgotten rooms always have the best kinds of darkness!"

As the Cheshire Cat finished his sentence, his tail slipped through his fingers and vanished completely.

She waited for him to go on, but he didn't.

"What does that have to do with Alice's house? Are we still talking about rooms, or about something else?" she asked impatiently. "Or are you trying to tell me that I'm standing in a room that I chose to forget?"

"You ask too many questions," he said, as he rolled his eyes and made his tail reappear. "Why don't you go find the truth for yourself?"

She gazed at the floating Cat for a moment. *Who knew a day would come when I would look to a floating cat for answers?* she wondered, not caring whether or not he intercepted her thought. "I guess you're right," she said, this time aloud. "I don't need to spend another second in this garden, I need to find Alice's house. When I find her, I find answers. The answers that will lead me out of this meditation and back to my world. I'm ready."

"That's more like it! All you had to do was say so!" the Cheshire Cat choked out between fits of laughter. As his laugher grew, his head began to spin faster and faster like a top. "And before your head starts to spin in circles, remember what I told you. You find silence only in the absence of your mind, where there is Nothing. Not even You." He carried on with his fit as he held out his paw, one sharp claw pointed directly behind her.

Immediately she turned around to see the wall of thorns open up to reveal a crooked path that wound directly to a house that looked like an abandoned Victorian cottage. The house was just one story with two large windows that framed a black door nearly triple their size, as if it had small eyes and a gaping mouth that longed to eat her whole. She recognized the door to be the same one she saw Alice escape through at the end of the labyrinth at the bottom of the rabbit hole. Black vines snaked up its cracked, white stone walls like veins. Several of the windows were cracked, but she saw nothing but blackness behind the broken panes. The state of the windows reflected the rest of the decayed house. Several slates had broken off of the light blue roof that matched the color of Alice's dress, and the white stone was cracked and blackened in many places. There was a single brick chimney that appeared to be caving in on itself, cracking under the pressure of the vines that were slowly taking over it and the rest of the house. It looked to Elizabeth as if it had once been a charming country home, but now it seemed to be crumbling, consumed by the darkness that slithered up its walls.

Suddenly, she remembered her talk with the raven from the meadow courtyard: *"A blue-and-white house, far, far away, with a garden of strange wildflowers, wildflowers like we've never seen before. We've only seen it once, and it had an odd feeling about it. It's very dark where it is."* Before her stood that house, Alice's house, which gave her the very same odd feeling. She also remembered the way the raven had described the path here, which contained, *"Some twins, something floating, and horrible, noisy beings."* The raven's vision emerged from her mind and manifested itself before her.

Or was it my vision all along? she thought to herself. As she continued to take in Alice's house and its dark aura, her eyes fell upon the black door again, and she noticed something that she hadn't seen before. The door was cracked open several inches. "Cheshire, was that door open before? I could have sworn—"

She turned around to face the Cat, but he was gone.

"Cheshire Cat?"

There was no answer.

Yet she didn't feel alone for long, because she heard a faint rustling coming from a patch of flowers just ahead, near the front door of the house. She squared her stance and walked toward it with clenched fists. Her intrepidity got the best of her as she marched curiously toward the sound. The rustling stopped and started sporadically. When Elizabeth finally reached the trembling bed of flowers, she leaned down and brushed a thick patch of yellow wildflowers away with her hand.

She heard a scream as she uncovered a small hole, with a small brown face staring back at her with scared, black eyes. It was a badger.

"Sorry!" she said softly. "Don't be afraid, I didn't mean to scare you, I just heard a noise and thought—"

"You scared me half to death!" the badger panted, and Elizabeth muffled a laugh.

"Again, I'm sorry. My name is Elizabeth."

"It's rude to laugh at someone who's frightened, you know."

"Tell me about it," she mumbled under her breath.

"So if you don't mind, Elizabeth," she squeaked. "I'll be going now—"

"Wait! Don't go yet. What's your name? I'm not going to hurt you, just a quick question and I'll be on my way, promise."

The badger stared at her with one eye open and the other closed, always keeping her body mostly hidden within her burrow. "Ava," the badger replied.

"Ava!" she said more to herself than to the badger.

"Yes, that's me, I'm just waiting for my husband to get home. He's been gone a very long time. So if you don't mind—"

"I met your husband, actually! Earlier today!"

"You did?" the badger said, as she poked her head all the way out of her burrow.

"I ran into him in a meadow courtyard just outside of the woods. There was a floating tree and many other animals, and—"

"I knew it!" Ava yelled, her eyes suddenly welling with anger. "He promised he would take me out, and there he goes and gets himself lost in his own thoughts! No follow-through," she mumbled to herself.

"I'm sorry to hear that," Elizabeth said, afraid she was losing Ava to her own thoughts before she could get her question out. "Anyway, do you know who lives in that house? Do you know if she's home now?"

Ava stared at her blankly, with one eye still closed.

"I'm talking about the girl in the blue dress."

At this question, Ava's eyes became very wide, and her mumbling stopped cold.

"I need to find her. Alice, I mean. The girl who lives there."

Ava's gaze remained wide, fixed on a spot behind Elizabeth.

"Ava?" Elizabeth asked as she realized she had lost her. For a moment, she considered taking out her compact again, tempted to use it as she had on the raven to break the tiny badger out of the prison of her own thoughts. Instead, she turned around to see what Ava was staring at.

On the crooked dirt path behind her, a letter waited.

"Thanks," Elizabeth said abruptly, as she left the badger, whose eyes still hung on the white, folded piece of paper that looked identical to the one she received before she went through the black door the first time. Across the front of the envelope was an inscription written in sprawling cursive that read *OPEN ME.*

She crawled over to the letter and picked it up, yet something made her freeze before she could begin to wipe the dirt off. Beneath the letter was Alice's footprint in the dirt path.

"She's home," Elizabeth whispered, as she eyed the outline of the familiar round ballet flat.

She looked down the path and saw more of Alice's footprints, which seemed jaggedly and widely spaced apart, as if she had been staggering sloppily with each step. The footprints led directly to the cracked, black door of the house, which now stood wide open. Elizabeth tried to gulp, but all at once her thoughts were grasping at her throat to escape.

How did she get around me without me seeing her?

She turned her attention back to the letter, which was now wet from her palms. The envelope ripped jaggedly at the seams. Her eyes were hungry to take in Alice's words, but to her surprise, she couldn't immediately read it because the letters were written backward.

"Strange," Elizabeth said, as she painstakingly tried to translate it for herself. She turned it from side to side and tried to make out each word. "She wrote every letter backward? Like they're mirrored!" Elizabeth sighed in frustration. *I knew she wouldn't make this easy. How did she have time to write this and leave it behind me? I didn't hear anything!*

She continued to turn the letter in her hands, as she tried to decipher each word, and then she felt the weight in her back pocket.

"Is this why she gave me my compact? Like she knew this whole time that every step of the journey was leading up to this letter."

She pulled the compact from her pocket and held it to the script. She slowly scanned it over each line. She read the letter in the reflection of the glass:

It's about time! But remember, you haven't caught me yet.

How did you like my garden? I noticed you looked a little pale. The rabbits weren't your cup of tea?

Also, I'm beginning to think you're obsessed with me. The way you talk about me to everyone, the way you see my face everywhere. It's like you're in love with me or something! And just so you know, it makes you look a little pathetic. But that's just so, terribly YOU.

By the way, you owe me a new mask. I saw you shatter my old one.

What are you waiting for? Are you ready to come in and play? I left the door open for you. You don't have to knock. You're already in.

—Alice

Twelve

Elizabeth crumpled the letter in her fist, prepared for a fight. Her eyes remained fixed on the house. Her heart pounded in her chest, as she shoved the paper in her back pocket with the rest of Alice's letters. Without looking behind her, she marched on toward the unknown. The dirt on the path Elizabeth walked on began to crack underneath her boots. Carefully, she put her foot on Alice's footprint and jumped from print to print as plumes of dust rose up behind her.

Elizabeth's staggering was interrupted only when she reached the stairs leading to Alice's front door, though it was not the decaying, decrepit steps that made her pause. The flame-like wildflowers did not reach up to the front porch, but rather stopped to reveal a scene that Elizabeth recognized from the meadow courtyard when she first laid her eyes on the inverted tree. Here the same tree floated before her, in the clearing in front of Alice's house of horrors, floating upside down. Though it was still difficult to tell the tree's roots from its branches, she could see that a light snow rested on the jagged top branches—or roots. The white snow on the black bark made the roots look like daggers, glinting in the dimming twilight of the moonless Wonderland sky.

She marveled at the tree for a few moments, and then her gaze fell to her feet, which were planted firmly at the outskirts of a wide puddle. The puddle reflected the tree, allowing her to see the tree right side up in the mirrored water.

It was upside down all along. I can't believe I didn't see it before.

The snow clearly lay at the tree's sharp roots, and, for the first time in a long time, the image she saw in the water looked natural. Her gaze swam in the calm water. She thought to herself that maybe it's not our reflections that scare us— maybe it's the truth. She saw the tree, clearly upside down and floating like the tree in the meadow courtyard, yet the water's reflection showed the reality of the vision. The truth had been staring back at her the whole time.

Next to the tree's reflection her face blurred in the murky water. She could have lost herself in it for a moment, if it had not been for the creaking of the large black door of Alice's house, agitated by an invisible breeze in the night. With determination, Elizabeth collected herself and took a deep breath. She knew the time for confrontation had come, and she was determined to find the truth that waited for her in Alice's lair.

Before she proceeded, she took one look behind her, letting herself fully absorb how far she'd come. The twisted walls of thorns stretched out before her, bending like barbed wire against the fiery flowerbeds, with the small watering cans flitting in the distance like strange mechanical hummingbirds. She saw herself in each thorn and in each petal. She saw herself in the tree before her and looked up to see small snowflakes begin to fall from the blackened sky. Just like the roots of the floating oak tree, she too became covered in snow. Yet the snowflakes did not feel cold on her bare skin, nor did they melt.

"Alice, I'm ready. I'm finally ready," she said, after taking another deep breath. She brushed the snowflakes off her shoulder. There was no trace of the scrape on her shoulder from the thorns. As she marched up the stairs of the porch, the steps creaked under her feet, as if they hadn't been climbed in a long time. For a moment, she feared that the wood would splinter under her feet, and then she saw the faint dirt outline of Alice's round shoe on the top step.

"Always two steps ahead of me," Elizabeth sighed. "But that's about to change. One more corner, one more door, and then you're mine," she whispered, as her fingertips traced the cracked black paint on the door. *I guess there's no reason to knock?* She straightened out invisible wrinkles in her shirt, as she paused to hear any sounds that might be stirring within.

Hearing nothing, she uttered one nervous, cracked laugh at the absurdity of her own thought.

"Knock. As if that would make a difference," she said aloud, nearly laughing at herself. "I must really be losing my mind." She bit the inside of her lip and reached for the doorknob.

Slowly, she pushed the door open, feeling a sharp pain in her forehead with each creak of the door. A tightness released in her chest, as she gasped. For a moment, she'd forgotten to breathe. She closed her eyes and stepped inside, closing the door behind her. Once she heard the clicking of the door, she opened her eyes again to find herself alone in a room that was nearly dark, except for a hanging lightbulb in the center of the entryway. It hung on a long wire and swung slowly back and forth like a pendulum, as if someone had just run through the room and disturbed its slumber. As the lightbulb swung back and forth it let out high-pitched creaks, like it was screaming to break free from the wall. Even in the dim light, she saw spiderwebs in all corners of the room and black shades that lined the broken windows behind her. There were only two pieces of furniture in the room: a white side table, like the one Elizabeth found at the end of the marble labyrinth, and an overturned chair that rested on its back just underneath the screaming lightbulb. Two rabbit's ears were carved into the spine of the white wooden chair. The cushions were streaked with dust, but Elizabeth imagined that in good condition the white rabbit chair must have looked like a throne.

Yet nothing held Elizabeth's gaze as long as the object that sat on top of the white side table, an object that had not been there before, when she had originally seen the table and retrieved Alice's first note in the marble labyrinth. On top of the table sat a toppled clock, which looked identical to the clock that she left face down on the desk near her Buddha statue.

She reached out and turned it right side up. In the place of numbers the word "NOW" was printed twelve times around the clock's face, which also lacked hands.

How did it get here? Elizabeth wondered, as she stroked its face with her fingertip.

She thought to herself that the entry of the house looked like an interrogation room for the mentally insane. *This is definitely Alice's house.*

A particularly loud scream coming from the lightbulb distracted her musings. She glanced over her shoulder and saw that it continued its crooked dance above the overturned chair, still screeching and casting shadows on the spiderwebs in the corners of the room, distracting her from the state of the front door. Nail marks streaked the surface of the door, but she hadn't seen scratch marks on the outside.

Someone tried to claw their way out of the house from the inside.

This door mirrored another black door across the room from it, which lead to the rest of the house, though it lacked the desperate abrasions near its rusted doorknob.

"Someone must have been trapped here!" she gasped, as she put down the clock and ran back to the front door, which was inexplicably locked. She tugged at the doorknob until she pulled it out of the doorframe. She stared at it for a moment, cradling it in her glistening palm. She let it fall to the floor, as the realization sunk in that she was not completely trapped. The second door beckoned her from across the room, mocking her with its unscratched black paint. "More doors. Of course, there are more doors," she muttered. Before crossing the creaky floor, she turned to face the white side table again and gave its top drawer a tug. *If she wants to send me a final letter, this is where it would be. Right where the first one was,* she thought. *The letter that led me into this nightmare.*

She struggled to open the drawer, quickly discovering that it had been glued shut. She traced the edges with her fingers. In some places the glue was still wet.

"She's been one step ahead of me this whole time!" she

shouted in frustration, kicking the leg of the table so hard that it cracked, causing the rest of the table to buckle and crash to the floor. The clock smashed face down against the ground, shattering into a pile of NOWs. "I know you heard that, Alice! I'm here, so you might as well show yourself! What else do you want to lock shut, psycho?"

Elizabeth's words bounced off the walls and echoed back at her, yet she still heard nothing from the rest of the house, except for the lightbulb still screaming in the background.

"If you thought you could break me by getting crafty with that stupid table, you thought wrong! And guess what? I'm not leaving. So, you might as well come out and show yourself now, or else the rest of your house is going to look like this table by the time I walk back out of that door! You know you're not even that clever, leaving notes and following me everywhere I go, like my life is some kind of sick, twisted game played out for your own entertainment! It's like you're the one who's obsessed with me! This may be your playground, but I'm not playing by your rules. Not anymore."

As she struggled to catch her breath, the silence of the room seemed to grow louder. The silence felt like company, the friendly, beckoning wave of mystery. The lightbulb's creaking had stopped, as if the house changed with the little whispers of her nightmares. After she regulated her breath, Elizabeth began to channel her anger into focus as she kicked the remains of the table out of her path, strode across the creaking floor, and wildly grabbed the doorknob of the second door. She pulled it open so hard that its hinges nearly gave out, and she closed it so harshly behind her that it hung slightly crooked on its doorframe.

Stretched out before her was a long corridor that reminded her of the labyrinth that led her to Alice in the first place. The long, dark hallway ended with yet another door. This one stood crookedly ajar, just like the one behind her. She could just make out a faint light emanating from the room, drawing her forward. As she took a step, she heard something shatter and immediately looked down at her feet. The floor of the long hallway was made out of thousands of shards of broken glass, all glued together with some jagged ends sticking out haphazardly. With each step she took, she heard more shattering as the glass broke into more shards. Their song mesmerized her. Elizabeth was so taken by the echo of the glass beneath her feet that she did not notice the mirror frames that hung all down the walls of the hallway, though no mirrors hung within them. The skeleton frames hung at all different heights and widths along the wall. It was as if the mirrors had died suddenly, fallen out of their frames, and crashed to the floor to become whole again in a sea of fragments.

She looked down at the aisle of broken mirrors and crouched to see her reflection. Her distorted and fractured face glared back at her from the shards; some glinted in the light coming from the cracked door ahead of her. In one piece, she could see her green right eye staring back at her, and the shard next to it showed half of her lips instead of her left eye, which blinked back at her from the shard where her forehead should have been.

She thought to herself that this hallway was like staring into an abstract self-portrait.

"If that portrait were hanging in a madhouse," she

mumbled. *By the looks of it, I'm pretty sure that's where I am. In Alice's asylum.*

More glass cracked beneath her boots, as she walked slowly forward, and she couldn't keep her eyes off of her broken image. She cracked one particularly large fragment in the center, and it split apart like serrated ripples in ice, though the cracks only covered her face. In the place of her eyes, nose, and lips was a jagged spiral pattern, with the center ripple forming just in between her eyes. *I'm beginning to look like the Cheshire Cat*, she thought, remembering the tribal pattern of orange stripes on his forehead. She clenched her jaw and hoped she wouldn't lose her head.

By the time she looked up from the floor, she was only a few steps away from the door. Light still shone from the cracks where the large black frame hung ajar. For a moment, she thought she saw a shadow quickly move past the door, shutting out the light for a second.

She wondered if she had just blinked, or if someone had slid past the door from the other side.

"Alice, are you in there?" she asked, this time louder. Her call was met with silence. "Fine. I guess I'll just have to come in there and see you for myself!" As she forced out the last few words, the space in the middle of her forehead began to burn more than ever before, as if the hidden eye had opened. She rubbed her forehead tenderly with her fingers, mustering all of her strength. "Knock, knock, bitch!" she said firmly, as she rose and pushed the door with all of her force.

A thick curtain of darkness enveloped Elizabeth.

What happened to the light I saw coming through the door? she thought, as her fingers searched blindly along the wall for a switch. *There has to be a light! Please . . . light!*

Suddenly, a dim light arose, though she couldn't tell from where. She found herself alone, surrounded by mirrors. It looked like a house of mirrors, but not quite like the ones you find in carnivals. Alice's house was more than that.

She stood in the middle of what seemed like hundreds of paneled mirrors, and her reflection appeared to stretch for miles behind her. Her tall, lean body reflected off of each mirror onto another, so in some reflections she stood with her back to herself. As she turned her head to find her bearings her mirrored reflection looked in all directions. Finally her eyes settled on one of the mirrors in the center of the room, and suddenly she felt thousands of eyes on her. They were all her own. Slowly she crept forward, and something disturbing manifested itself in each mirror she passed. In one she began to stare at herself, and the image of hands grabbing at her face stared back at her. The bony fingers covered one of her eyes, as another hand wrapped around her neck, and another pulled at her hair.

"Get off me, get off!" she screamed as she swatted at her face, though there was nothing there, "What kind of house of mirrors is—"

Her sentence was cut short as she came across a mirror as broad as she was tall, graffitied with a sprawling cursive handwriting. The words *I TOLD YOU TO RUN* were etched across the surface of the mirror with red lipstick, with *XOXO* written just underneath, curiously at her exact height.

"Real cute, Alice. You think you can scare me off like

when I fell down the rabbit hole? Well, keep up. I'm not running," she said as she walked passed the mirror next to it, which was cracked in some places. As she looked in the mirror she saw her face reflected in a hundred triangles, as the glass had cracked in a prism-like pattern. She stared into a perfect triangle with her face in the center, and then above it into another triangle where her face hung upside down. Fragments of herself surrounded her, thousands of Elizabeths in various shapes and forms stared back at her with curiosity. Her heart began to race and she felt hot beads of sweat drip down her forehead and the back of her neck. She wiped her palms on her thighs.

Suddenly she felt a thousand tiny, hot pinpricks at the back of her neck. Someone ran their fingers through her hair.

"I dream of us together, a little dream I dream every night," sang a sultry voice from over Elizabeth's left shoulder. Each word was sung slowly, hanging in the air around her with every decadent syllable pronounced carefully, rolled over the tongue like rich honey, encircling her in an ever-tightening ring.

Elizabeth spun around to face the singer but saw only her own reflection from one of the mirrors.

"Alice?"

"Wondering if you dream of me too," the voice sang, with each word sounding more sinister than the last.

"I know it's you, Alice!" Elizabeth shouted, as she started pushing against the mirrors around her. "Come out and—"

"Because for better or worse, I think we might—"

"Stop!" Elizabeth screamed. She covered her ears to escape the sound of the echoes of the voice around her. "Give it up already," she shouted, choking out the words between breaths. "I didn't come all the way here to listen to your creepy—"

"*Be together forever,*" the sultry voice rang out once more, dragging out the last syllable of the word "forever," as if it were being said to someone learning English for the first time, letting the strong "F" sound fade to the purr of a long "R."

Then, a sharp, bottomless silence.

Elizabeth backed herself against the mirror behind her and uncovered her ears, letting her arms hang by her sides.

"Calm down, just breathe," she panted to herself. "It's just your mind playing tricks on you. They're only mirrors, they can't hurt you."

"No," said the smooth, deep voice. "But I can. You're in my house now, bitch."

Instantly, she felt as if an avalanche of rocks rolled down her spine. It was as if she were a human rainstick, one of the wooden toys she had as a child with rocks inside that made the sound of falling rain when turned upside down.

"Alice!"

"For a minute I didn't think you'd show up. It's about time," Alice said.

At the sound of the cracked, disturbed voice Elizabeth jumped, and her back slammed against one of the mirrors behind her. She heard the mirror crack in a few places. She turned around to face it and saw a pair of legs adorned with white tights and black ballet flats where her own legs stood.

"Alice!" she screamed again. "Where are you? Stop hiding! Are you scared?" Elizabeth turned around to face her, but realized that she stood alone. She darted quickly to some of the mirrors around her, trying to look behind them or to find a dark corner where Alice could be hiding.

"Oh, so you finally want to see me, then? Are you sure you're ready? Because you were really taking your sweet time before."

"I'm ready. More ready than I've ever been. Come out, you freak!"

"Wow, that hurts. Have any more harsh digs? Pretty big words for such a little girl," Alice's smooth voice coaxed. "I think you're the one who's scared. I think you're a pathetic, frightened little girl. Just like you've always been."

"You're wrong, Alice. That's not me. Not anymore."

"Oh? Is that why you're sweating like a pig? It's not a good look, you know. No wonder Adam is having second thoughts about you."

"Second thoughts?" Elizabeth said, almost to herself. "You're a liar! Don't go there. Don't even start! I know what you're doing. You're trying to make me doubt myself. You don't know him!"

"Sweetie, I know him better than you think."

As Elizabeth took in Alice's words, still searching every corner, her vision was overtaken by an image of Alice and Adam lying together on the living room sofa in Adam and Elizabeth's apartment. Alice's head rested in Adam's lap, as he stroked her long, blonde hair.

"Get out of my head!"

"You're in your own head."

"That's not true! You've been manipulating me this whole time," Elizabeth cried as she shook her head. "You're making all of it up. You only showed me that to scare me!"

"And I think it's working."

"Have you been stalking me this entire time?" Elizabeth yelled, as she remembered lazy afternoons when she cuddled with Adam on their couch in that exact same position. "Have you been in my apartment, watching me? How do you get in?"

"Don't act so high and mighty! I was invited. You let me in yourself. Don't you remember?"

Another image flashed before Elizabeth's mind. This time it was the black velvet pouch that rested behind her perfume bottle.

"What are you saying?"

"*This is the way my life ends,*" Alice taunted in a tone that made it sound like she was reading a bedtime story to a child. "*This is the way my life ends, not with a light, but lost in darkness.* Should I wipe my sweaty palms on my pants and bite my lip, too?"

Elizabeth crossed her arms tightly against her chest.

"Come on, I know you're not as stupid as you look," Alice's voice boomed. "Don't make me repeat myself. You let me in, remember? If you really want the truth maybe it's time you really look at me, if you're so brave. Step up to the mirror, sweetheart, take a look for yourself!" Alice said, as she erupted in a fit of laughter from somewhere in the darkness.

Suddenly, the dim lights in the room faded, leaving only one light above the mirror in the center of the room. Elizabeth stepped toward it cautiously, unsure of exactly what she might find.

"I can do this," she said to herself with a strong voice. *I'm ready.*

As she stepped in front of the mirror before her, she took a sharp breath and looked herself in the eye. She held the gaze, but it began to change before her eyes. In the reflection, she saw her head split in two. At first, the head on the left was a mirror image of the one on the right, but then the features began to morph. On her left head the black hair turned almost white, and then settled into a light blonde. The green eyes turned translucent and then into a sky blue. Next to her head rested Alice's head, both attached to her own body. Elizabeth held the gaze but stepped back slowly, taking in her full reflection, which continued to change like a kaleidoscope of her own image. As quickly as it had appeared, Alice's head faded away, leaving Elizabeth's body intact again, but only for a moment. And then suddenly, Alice's reflection replaced her own. Finally, they stood face to face in the mirror.

"There you are! Why don't you come out and play?" Elizabeth said in a deep, smooth voice. She moved closer to the mirror and reached out to touch Alice's reflection.

As soon as she moved closer, standing eye to eye with Alice's reflection, the reflection changed again, to that of her own. She found herself staring deep into her own green eyes. Gone were the two black voids she had seen in the mirror on her medicine cabinet, the ones she tried to face each day. The deeper she looked, the more she saw a faint darkness that seemed to coexist with the light.

"Were they both there before?" she said, as she stepped back, still marveling at her own image, eager to take in her full reflection. But to her surprise, her own reflection began to come to life. Though she stood still, she watched her reflection in the mirror move on its own, as if she stood in front of a movie screen.

First, Elizabeth saw herself sitting on her knees, writing frantically on a piece of paper, pausing occasionally to quickly glance over her shoulder. When Elizabeth caught the eye of her reflection they were not green, but a light blue. They stared fixedly at one another, until Elizabeth's reflection, who had just folded the note, pressed her index finger to her lips and whispered, "Shh!"

Then the image blurred, and she saw herself hiding a letter in the top drawer of a white side table in a dark marble corridor. Elizabeth watched herself running alongside hedgerows filled with roses, and she stopped to hide a piece of paper at the bottom of one of the hedges.

The image began to blur and take a new form again, this time replaying Elizabeth's first conversation with the Cheshire Cat. "*I'm looking for Alice*," she heard her voice say within her mind as she watched her reflection mouth the words, and she watched the Cat's patterned forehead furrow for the second time. Then, suddenly, as the view of the Cat's face began to pan outward, Elizabeth saw Alice standing before him in her place. "*Why are you looking for her?*" she watched the Cat ask Alice as she heard his familiar voice replay in her mind.

Then, as the reflection changed again, she saw herself standing before a clearing in a forest, watching a butterfly holding a blue pill on one wing and an orange pill on the other float in the mirrors on all sides of her.

The image of the butterfly grew fuzzy and disappeared, only to be replaced by the reflection of herself rolling a mirror behind a sleeping willow tree. The reflection shifted again, this time showcasing Tweedle Dee and Tweedle Dum with horror-stricken expressions frozen on their faces before they disappeared. Then she watched herself run away from the scene, through the woods, stopping before a wall of hanging branches to pick white threads out of her back pocket. Carefully, she tied the strings together to fasten a note to a protruding stick in the wall.

The reflection took on a sepia tone as the image faded, like she was watching an old movie. Finally, the reflection returned to full color as she watched Tweedle Dum standing beneath the willow tree addressing her during their second encounter. *"Oh yes, I've seen her! Your twin!"* she heard in her mind, as Tweedle Dum mouthed the words on the glass surface, which began to turn black as he disappeared.

The black surface began to vibrate as she heard the Mad Hatter's shrieks ringing through her mind, calling Alice's name as Elizabeth ran away from his tea party. *"Alice! Alice!"*

Finally, the mirror stopped shaking. It began to glow as colors swirled on its surface. Slowly, the colors came together to reveal Elizabeth standing in Alice's garden, surrounded by broken porcelain rabbits, makeup, and tiaras. The Cheshire Cat's image began to form again in the mirror's reflection, but in the place of his orange cat form he appeared as a bright white light.

"Honestly, you're completely mad. You put them there. They're yours, of course!" She heard his words reverberate through her mind as the mirror changed to reflect the mask of her face in the tangled grass. Elizabeth saw her reflection standing before

her with the mask of her own face on. For a moment, she thought the image was frozen, until she watched as her reflection reached up to rip the mask off. The mask crashed to the grassy floor, breaking into shards of porcelain, revealing Elizabeth standing there with piercing blue eyes and blonde hair.

She continued to stare at the mirror with her hand covering her mouth, as the image of Alice's face on her own body faded to black. The reflection of the mirror began to rewind and fast-forward in a choppy way, as if her thoughts were a movie that lost its sense of direction. She witnessed a montage of herself writing letters, painting on wooden signs, and hiding in trees and thick grasses to watch herself from afar. The last image reflected in the montage was of Elizabeth walking up the stairs to Alice's house, leaving a dusty, round footprint in the shape of a ballet flat on the top step.

She stared at her reflection in the mirror. She blinked and saw herself in a sky blue dress, Alice's wild blue eyes staring back at her, a half grin spreading across her face. She blinked again, and Elizabeth saw herself again, but this time with a lingering light in her eyes that she hadn't seen before.

"I'm you," Elizabeth said as her hand fell from her mouth. "I'm Alice."

"A prize for the winning guess!" she heard Alice's screech echo in her mind.

"It was me all along? I was the one leaving myself letters? I led myself through Wonderland the whole time?"

"I guess you aren't as dumb as you look."

"And that's how you read my mind. You were me all along. Your thoughts were my thoughts!"

"Me, me, me. God, you're vain," Alice's voice interjected from the void.

You created this place. You created everything in it. Alice's words, her words, echoed through her mind yet again.

"We're both bad, you know. We're wicked." Alice's voice rang in her mind as Elizabeth continued to look herself in the eye.

Elizabeth closed her eyes and saw herself, with Alice's blue eyes, telling a teenage Adam to leave. The ice in those blue eyes then flashed at a faceless blonde boy she never knew, who left her feeling empty, kissing his lips as any thoughts of Adam vanished from her mind. She saw Alice, with her long, blonde hair, holding hands with this blonde boy until she pushed him away, too. Then her eyes softened back to green and locked on Adam's green eyes, which were somehow darker than before. Hurt spread out from the light green irises in splashes of forest green. She opened her eyes and the vision left her, breaking apart into a flock of black ravens that flew off into the darkness.

She blinked hot tears away.

"That's what happens when you lock me away!" Alice continued, "You hurt the ones you love, and you hurt yourself. You're not better than me. You never were. In fact, let's be honest, you're nothing without me!"

"And you're nothing without me!" Elizabeth shot back with renewed courage, "Don't forget that! You're a part of me. I came here to look you in the eye, and I need your respect. You're not going to destroy me."

"Not yet anyway."

As Alice's voice trailed from her mind, Elizabeth saw

moving images stare back at her from the mirror one again, though faster this time. She saw herself throw her tooth-brush in the sink, she saw herself swallow the orange pill with the *20* stamped across the front, and she saw herself fighting with Adam, pushing him away with a cold stare.

"No more pills. I promise. I don't need to lock you away anymore," she said to her own reflection as her forehead burned again, "I'm awake now. And you know what else? I feel sorry for you."

With these words, the mirrors began to shake as the ground rumbled beneath her, but Elizabeth's voice carried on stronger than ever.

Alice said nothing.

"You heard me! I feel sorry for you, hiding away down here like a forgotten child!"

Suddenly, the room began to shake so hard that for a moment Elizabeth thought it might fall to pieces, and as the room began to rumble more and more violently her voice, too, began to quake.

"Alice," Elizabeth said as tears began to well up in her eyes, blurring her vision. "When did I lose you?" She thought of her Alice doll, the one from her childhood, collecting dust upon her shelf near the spot where she meditated. "When did I push you away? Why did I lock you down here in the dark-ness, waiting for me to find you again?"

"Your tears mean nothing to me, bitch." She heard Alice's dark, smooth voice reverberate through her mind. "You said it yourself. You forgot about me. But I won't let that happen again." The room lurched violently back and forth, which caused Elizabeth to nearly lose her balance and fall on the cracking floor. "Sometimes the journey of awakening to who we really are isn't all light and rainbows. Sometimes it's dark. Sometimes it's just like experiencing your whole life shatter to pieces, but then realizing that it was only a mirror that shattered—"

"—Only a reflected image of my self," Elizabeth finished.

"Yes," Alice's dark, seductive voice went on, "You were always the one seeing the reflection, and until now you mistook your reflection to be who you are. Like that stupid tree outside."

As Elizabeth uttered Alice's last words, the mirror in front of her began to splinter. The first crack struck through Elizabeth's forehead, splitting her face in two. The left half of her face had black hair, porcelain skin, and green eyes, but the right side of her face had long, blonde hair and striking blue eyes. With another loud crack, the mirror shattered and fell to pieces on the floor.

Suddenly, the other mirrors followed suit, some slowly and others quickly, all shattering to the ground around her. Shards of glass exploded and flew through the air, whizzing by her in a blur, as the room began to turn black, barely missing her.

At the start she saw only darkness, and in the darkness a mirror hung, waiting, she heard Alice's voice in her head echo over the shattering of the house of mirrors. She looked frantically around her for a way out, for a way to come out of her meditation before this world fell to pieces.

Then, a light gazed into that mirr—

The sound of the broken glass hitting the floor was nearly

deafening, but Elizabeth heard Alice's words loud and clear as a light began to appear above her, where the tall mirror used to stand.

The glow of a single flame reflected in an infinite looking glass.

Elizabeth felt the floor begin to crack and rumble beneath her, as if it too were a mirror about to splinter into a thousand tiny pieces. At any second she felt that the ground would open up and swallow her whole into its black, gaping mouth. It shifted like tectonic plates, giving Elizabeth no choice but to scramble across the cracking floorboards like a crab trying to steady herself, digging into the floor with her heels.

The mirror with Alice's, or Elizabeth's, final warning stood erect, and the lipstick melted off of its surface, dripping to the floor in a pool of red as if it were bleeding out. Finally it crumbled to the floor.

As this flame gazed at her reflection, she not only saw the light, she also saw the darkness, and she knew that it was good.

Elizabeth began to regain her strength, as she made eye contact with her reflection in a shard of glass that flew past her face. She closed her eyes and took several deep breaths, allowing her breath to ground her just as it had when she started her meditation.

So she desired more of herself to be unveiled by the light. She let herself blaze brighter into the mirror . . .

She felt her entire body becoming hot, emanating from within. Shards of mirror whizzed around her, but none of them touched her. She held up her right hand and watched a jagged piece of glass pass right through it.

Brighter, and brighter . . . Alice's voice continued, unshaken.

Elizabeth heard the sound of more glass breaking around her as her own inner light took over her, coming from within and transcending outward. The light seemed to emit from her wounds, the invisible scrapes on her shoulders from where the thorns in Alice's garden had cut her. The shards reflected the light beaming all around her, sending it up to the ceiling and letting it fall back down upon her. As she found herself immersed in a pool of her own inner light, she felt herself slowly slipping away.

Until the potency of her light shattered the mirror. Alice's booming voice continued from inside her mind.

Suddenly the shattering stopped, and billions of shards of glass flying in every direction froze in midair. Elizabeth looked around her and saw herself in each shard, her face multiplied by the millions. The broken mirrors magnified the light coming from within her.

In the beginning there was darkness, and in the end, a million rays of light.

With Alice's last words, Elizabeth found herself completely enveloped in her own light, blinking her eyes at the blinding white light all around her.

Thirteen

Elizabeth opened her eyes slowly, and her head ached, as she thought she heard Fitz's barks fill her ears.

"Ellie?"

She rubbed her eyes and gulped a few deep breaths. The first sight she saw as her eyes regained focus was her Alice doll, which sat on the shelf smiling back at her. She gazed at the Alice doll, acknowledging her, that little figure with her layer of dust and long shadow standing like a belated visitor at the end of a narrow corridor. For a moment, she swore she saw a light in the doll's eyes, accompanied by a familiar, twisted grin. Elizabeth returned the smile, and whispered to herself triumphantly, "Alice, we're home."

She felt the warmth of the sun streaming in through the windows, patting her shoulder like an old friend. She felt warmth, she felt home. The way home is supposed to feel.

She caressed the yoga mat beneath her, its pink surface looking brighter than ever before. Finally, she realized that the voice she just heard, the one that accompanied the chorus of Fitz's barks, was Adam's.

"Ellie?" he called again, "I hope I'm not interrupting your meditation, but I heard you start to move so—"

"Adam!" she cried with relief, turning to face him and lighting up at the sight of him smiling back at her from the kitchen. "You have no idea how much I missed you!"

His voice pulsed around her like a second heartbeat. She longed to jump up and run to him, but her eyes still burned a little as she took in the scenery and the brightness of their small apartment, which seemed to turn colors as her sight adjusted back to the real world. She turned to look at the clock that still sat face down on the desk, just as she had left it. She quickly crawled over to it and turned it right side up. She was relieved to see numbers and hands on its face.

"Missed me? You were only meditating for a few minutes!" Adam replied over the sound of clanging pots and pans.

For a moment, Elizabeth's heart nearly stopped as she recalled the last time she came out of her meditation. *Or, at least I thought I came out of it,* Elizabeth thought to herself. But this time, her knees ached from sitting in the lotus position, and her lower back stung from holding it in a straight posture. *Or did it ache from when I slammed against the mirror?*

She rubbed the center of her forehead.

"Adam, is this really our apartment?" she said, as her eyes searched the room. She smiled at the sight of chipped paint around the door.

"Are you okay?"

"I'm better than okay! I've never been so happy to see a stack of bills, piled high . . . And my old cooking magazines!" The sense of home filled her with the kind of warmth that makes you lock Doubt and Worry out for good, letting the key disappear into the folds of time. She couldn't keep herself from Adam a second longer.

"All right, please tell me what's wrong with you," Adam asked with a laugh and her favorite half smile.

She jumped to her feet, scooped up Fitz, and skipped over to Adam. The familiar butterflies began to dance in her stomach, as she looked into his green eyes. Her arms loosened, and Fitz jumped to the floor and trotted away.

Elizabeth wrapped her arms around Adam's neck and pulled him to her, letting her lips find the familiar fold between his. She knew exactly how they fit together, his hands gripping her hips, their chests rising and falling against one another, like they had each other's bodies memorized. He smelled like fresh linen and oranges. His smell was comfort, his smell was home. She slid her hands down to his waist and fumbled her fingers under his shirt. Her fingers climbed up his side, touching his tattoo without seeing it.

She kissed him so hard he grabbed the kitchen counter behind him for balance. Then he fit his hands around her hips again and pulled her tighter against him. She let her hands slide down his back and around his belt, her fingers grazing the cold metal of the buckle as she let out a sigh.

His hands squeezed her hips and pushed her back so he could look into her eyes.

"That must have been some meditation!" he said, as he caught his breath.

She smiled back at him and smoothed down the side of his hair that was still sticking up. Fitz barked from his place under the small dining table. She turned to him and noticed the photo of her and Adam at the beach, with their normal green eyes staring back at her. A few high school photographs were still absent from their collection of memories on the shelves. She let her jaw relax as their flaws wrapped their big, warm arms around her and welcomed her home.

But there was still one place she had to check.

"Just one sec," she said with a smile, giving him one more kiss before walking away, "I just need to check—"

She tripped over Adam's sneakers, as she approached the bathroom where the medicine cabinet still hung.

"The medicine cabinet's still there!"

"Where else would it be? Really, Ellie, will you tell me what's going on? What could have possibly happened in your five minutes of meditation?"

"Just one more sec!" she replied as she walked into the bathroom and quietly shut the door behind her. *There's just one last thing I need to see for myself,* she thought.

Elizabeth flung open the medicine cabinet, and the creak of the door echoed against the walls of the small bathroom. She tossed aside her perfume bottle to reveal her black, velvety pouch where two remaining pills waited for her. Without hesitation, she threw them into the toilet and flushed.

For a brief moment, she saw an image flash through her mind of Alice's dark, smiling face grinning back at her, leaving her with a wink.

Elizabeth smiled as her hands searched her back pockets, which were empty. She turned back to the medicine cabinet and shut it gently, finding herself confronted by her own reflection once again. She took herself in, feeling both the light and the darkness emitting from her eyes, and saw her own truth. She saw the wrinkles and the acne scars, but she also saw the freckles from summers past, and the way the lines of her eyes would crease a little when she smiled wide. She no longer measured her strength by discipline, by being in control, by shutting out thoughts, or by denying her emotions. She measured her strength in moments she felt connected, in situations she showed compassion and gave hugs and smiles, in the time she spent intently listening to those around her, and in how hard she loved.

She thought to herself that she had many different sides of herself, some light and some dark, but they were all just a part of her. All integrated together and all parts of a whole, deeper, inner light. When she leaned further toward her reflection she felt she could see the different parts all meshed together in the swirling green and flecks of yellow, and they looked whole.

"Finally!"

"Ellie?" she heard Adam call from beyond the door. "Are you talking to me?"

"No, just talking to myself!" she said. She realized how crazy that sounded, but she no longer cared. "Be right there!" She took one last glance at herself and smiled, appreciating her inner journey. Finally she flicked the light off, and left the bathroom to face Adam.

"I have so much to tell you, I don't know where to start," she said, as she shut the door behind her.

"How about you start at the beginning, continue to the

end, and then stop," Adam said with his half smile, as he took a seat on the couch and patted the cushion next to him. Fitz crawled into the space between Adam's feet, beckoning Elizabeth with his wide, panting smile. She scratched his ear before she took her place next to Adam. She gulped down a big breath and nearly choked on it.

"The beginning? Okay . . . First I was meditating, and then I was falling down this rabbit hole, a real rabbit hole, Adam," she said, speaking so quickly he had to lean in to catch each word. "And I thought I had lost myself in this rabbit hole but really I found myself there, in Wonderland, as I looked into Alice's eyes, which were really my eyes—"

"Slow down!" he said as he tucked a strand of hair behind her ear. "I can barely understand you when you speak at a thousand words per second."

"Sorry, I know this must sound so crazy, but I was in Wonderland!"

"Wonderland?"

"Well, it was sort of Wonderland, but really it was my own subconscious world that I created for myself in order to find Alice, or really to find myself, and—"

"Alice was there?"

"Yes, she was there, but she was really me all along! And Tweedle Dee and Tweedle Dum were there too, only they weren't real twins but mirror twins . . . kind of like us! And the Cheshire Cat was there, and the Mad Hatter!"

"Ellie, are you sure you're feeling okay? You were only sitting for a few minutes."

"It may seem like that to you, but to me it was like I was

gone for so long and learned so much it was like every meditation I've ever had all wrapped into one."

"Meditations in Wonderland, you mean," he said with a
raised eyebrow.

Fitz's large ears perked up.

Elizabeth knew everything she said might be lost on Adam
for the moment. She knew that we each have our own internal world to discover that only makes sense to us. She relaxed
her jaw and felt the warmth in her face start to cool down.
"Exactly! I know what it sounds like, but time doesn't exist
there. It does here, but it definitely doesn't in Wonderland,"
she continued. "But there were no King and Queen of Hearts,
and there was no White Rabbit, or at least not in the way I
expected, anyway."

"I guess we must be the King and Queen then," he smiled,
as he put his hand on her thigh.

"You know you're right, in a way. This may sound crazy
to you, but in a way we're all of them."

"We're Alice, too?"

"Well, I am. Or she's me."

She walked over to the Alice doll sitting on the shelf. She
picked her up, holding her gently in her hands. She set her
down next to the Buddha and the clock.

"I haven't seen you touch her since we moved in," Adam
said, "Why the new home?"

"It's a thank you," she said. *To the monster who didn't succeed
in swallowing me alive.*

She turned to face him only to catch him rubbing the back
of his neck.

"I'm trying to follow you," he said, "But you have to forgive me if it all sounds a little bit like nonsense."

"Yes!" she said as she moved to join him again on the couch. "That's exactly what it is! Nonsense is truth, and truth is nonsense."

"It must be," he laughed. "How can there be a Wonderland without a White Rabbit?"

Fitz barked in protest, reminding her that she was going to be late.

"Maybe you should tell me more about it later tonight? I think you'll be late for work."

"Oh, God. The studio!" Elizabeth shouted and looked at the clock. She completely forgot that this was the real world, that time existed here, and that she should have left for the subway a few minutes ago to catch her train.

"Relax, should I call them and tell them you'll be running late? Maybe you should take a sick day?" Adam asked, as he stood up and put his hands on her shoulders.

"No!" she said in a pitch far too high. "No. I'm fine, Adam. Really."

"Take some deep breaths. I'll grab your bag and get you some water."

"Wait! Hold on," she said as she reached out and touched his back to turn him back toward her. "I love you."

He leaned down and rested both of his hands on her knees to look into her eyes.

"I love you with everything I am, with every part of me."

His green eyes gazed deeply into hers, the light and dark greens blending together, and she felt like he truly saw every part of herself, almost as if for the first time.

"I know," he said softly. "I love you, too. All of you."

Then he reached his hand up and wrapped his fingertips around the hair behind her neck, tilting her head back to kiss her in a way that made her feel that they were one, as if her body were just an extension of his. She lifted her chin up to kiss him harder and wrapped her ankles behind his back to pull him in closer. She felt that he kissed her as if she were finally whole, and he could feel it. Like when he kissed her, he kissed every part of her.

"Don't be late!" he whispered, as he unwound her ankles from behind him and went to pick up her bag. "And don't forget, you owe me the rest of the story later."

"Of course," she replied, as she caught her breath, stood up, smoothed out her shirt, and headed for the door. She grabbed her bag and kissed him once more, and blew a kiss to Fitz, who had fallen asleep on the Persian rug.

"Ellie? Just one more thing."

"I really have to go!"

"About before, the talk we had before your meditation—"

"Don't worry about it," she said with a smile. "I figured it out on my own!"

"I definitely need to hear about that later," he said with a grin like a crescent moon. "If I meditate after you leave, will I find Wonderland, too?"

"It's not about finding Wonderland. It's about finding yourself," she said with a wink before she raced out the door and shut it gently behind her.

The crowded streets of New York City awaited her. But before she stepped out of the building onto the gum-spotted pavement, she paused by the front door and took out her compact to fix her hair, then a mascara smudge, and finally took in the entire reflection of her face.

"That's more like it," she said to herself. She clicked it shut, threw it into her bag, and joined the throngs of New Yorkers, as she headed toward the subway station.

But as she walked her thoughts began to walk astride her, catching up to her at last.

She thought about how light she felt as she walked, and wondered if that was what freedom felt like. She wondered if she could be the woman she wanted to be, the one who had it all together, like the kind of woman who knew exactly what to make for dinner on a Wednesday night. The woman who had read that book, who had seen that movie. The woman who was kind, not only to others but also to herself. The woman who always knew what to buy her boyfriend for his birthday, and who creased the edges of the paper when she wrapped it just before the grand finale of a tying a white silk bow on top. But also the woman who was real, who wasn't always in control, who shaved her calves and not her thighs when she was in a hurry, who would forget to put on lipstick or who would drop a glass and cry about it for no reason, only to pick herself back up and forgive herself for it with the tenderness of the mother she hoped she could be one day. She wanted to be the one who smiled at her flaws and winked at her thoughts, who could take herself exactly as she was.

Then she thought about the uppers swirling into the black hole of her toilet bowl, gone once and for all. She found herself not only in a crush of bodies navigating the sidewalk, but in a crush of her own thoughts as she tried to take in everything she experienced in Wonderland. As she walked along the sidewalk in a trance-like state, she found a new sense of comfort as one particular thought crossed her mind, which reminded her that Alice would always be with her.

She took a few deep breaths and let the cold New York City air flow down her lungs like mercury.

"*Consciousness is a mirror, a mirror reflecting mirrors,*" echoed one of her thoughts in a deep, sultry voice.

At this thought, Elizabeth began to focus her attention on all of the elements that made up the world around her, which seemed no more or less real than Wonderland. Puddles streaked across the gray pavement and reflected the tops of buildings and the blue sky above them. It was a pale sort of blue, a dreaming, drifting color. The shadows of people in the crowd moving around her cast a distorted image of themselves onto the wet ground below them, making them look like statues that were eight feet tall. The colors of their clothes also streaked across the wet sidewalk, making the gray pavement in the wetter places look like a sea of dancing colors. The world suddenly looked more beautiful than it ever had before. All of the colors made her happy, even the gray felt like a radiant and welcoming void.

Has it always looked like this? she thought to herself.

Elizabeth's thoughts quieted as she took in the sight of the cracked side of an old building next to her, which displayed a stretched out line of graffiti in cursive script that read, *NOTHING.*

The sight of it caused an image of Alice's fierce blue eyes to flash across her mind again, accompanied by the faint voice of the Cheshire Cat uttering words she couldn't quite make out. She stopped in her tracks for a moment, as the memories screamed out for attention like the neon signs of the buildings around her.

Suddenly, Elizabeth felt someone run into her shoulder, nearly turning her completely around, knocking her bag to the wet pavement. "Only surrender can give you what you're looking for," she heard a voice whisper.

"Watch it!" a muffled voice muttered angrily, as a tall man with a bright blue tie and a large umbrella continued past her.

The collision pulled Elizabeth out of her trance, and she crouched down to collect her bag and several papers that had fallen out of it, as well as the compact that rolled to a stop on the wet pavement a few feet in front of her.

As she stuffed the last of the papers back in her bag and reached for the compact, she looked up at the parting sea of legs in the crowd before her. For a moment, she caught sight of a pair of legs clad with black ballet flats, white stockings, and the hem of a sky blue dress.

Just as soon as the legs had appeared, they ran around her and disappeared into the crowd. Elizabeth grabbed her mirror, threw it in her bag, and leapt to her feet, her eyes searching the horde of commuters that slowly closed in on her like dense trees in a forest.

She began to run, pushing her way through the throngs with urgency, searching for Alice yet again, this time above the surface of her subconscious world.

"Excuse me," Elizabeth muttered to those she pushed by. "Sorry, pardon me."

After a minute of winding her way through the labyrinth of the crowd, she stopped, and a single thought manifested itself in her mind in a familiar, smooth voice:

"Home sweet home at last. Welcome to the real world, bitch."

I owe a debt of inspiration to Lewis Carroll, without whom this story wouldn't have been possible. This is far from the first *Alice*-inspired novel published, and the timelessness of his story ensures that it will also be far from the last. This novel manifested because I, like so many others before me, have been inspired by Carroll's story since childhood. And like Carroll's original Wonderland, this story evolved within me to become a world of its own.

I took creative license with the characters of his I chose to include. The ones excluded, however, still haunt the pages in their own way. Fitz, for example, is in his own way a reincarnation of the White Rabbit, as the way the willow tree impersonates the Red King.

A writer, at heart, is foremost an observer and a voracious reader. In that spirit, other writers much greater than I, in addition to Carroll, were a source of inspiration. The quote Elizabeth says in chapter two, "This is the way my life ends," is prompted by T. S. Eliot's poem "The Hollow Men."

The sepulchre reference mentioned in passing in chapter two is inspired by Joseph Conrad's *Heart of Darkness*, which also gave rise, in some respects, to the way darkness alters the environment in many of the late chapters of this book.

Vladimir Nabokov's words, "Do not be angry with the rain; it simply does not know how to fall upwards," gave impetus to the Cheshire Cat's remark in chapter seven, when he tells Elizabeth: "Don't be mad at the onion, it doesn't know how to roll backwards!"

The song that Adam and Alice both sang, in chapters nine and twelve, is a grateful nod to "Happy Together," written by Garry Bonner and Alan Gordon, released in 1967 by The Turtles, but in particular the cover by Filter.

Many of the elements of chapter nine were influenced by Neil Gaiman's *Coraline*, including the ways in which the eyes and general personas of the characters appear.

While the name "Alice" has roots in many languages and cultures, the Greek origin of the name can be derived from the Greek word *alethéa*, which means "truth." While that may or may not have weighed in on Carroll's original work, it holds relevance here.

As for the rest, this book is a work of fiction. Alice said, "Everyone wears masks here." So when it comes to any perceived kernels of truth within the text, they all have rabbit masks on. Any attempt to further excavate for facts undermines the essence of the word "fiction." Nonsense is truth, and truth is nonsense, as Elizabeth put it. Ultimately, like Wonderland, to question whether something truly exists or not is to miss the point entirely. As Carroll reminds us: "Imagination is the only weapon in the war against reality."

ACKNOWLEDGMENTS

I would like to honor everyone who has left their fingerprints on this book.

Thank you to the wonderful and imaginative team at Greenleaf Book Group: Hobbs Allison, Tyler LeBleu, Lindsey Clark, Diana Ceres, Kim Lance, Carrie Jones, Tanya Hall, Jodi Boyer, and Carly Cohen. Without your combined efforts, *Meditations in Wonderland* would still be just a blog. Thank you for your inexhaustible support and for giving this book a home. Hobbs, thank you for taking a chance on me and bringing this book to life.

Thanks to everyone at Media Connect for your encouragement and guidance as I went from book publicist to first-time author.

Also, a big thank you to Professor Chris Boucher, who didn't call me crazy when I first walked into his office my senior year at Boston College, the first Friday of spring classes, in my beat up Nirvana t-shirt, blazer, and jeans and said, "I want to write a book." This book was only possible with your help and with your fiction workshop. Thanks for supervising my first tumble down the rabbit hole. Thank you to those who shared the class with me, for the gentle encouragement you gave, and for putting up with reading a full chapter during peer review sessions. Your comments were constructive and imperative, and you weren't as mean to me as Alice is to Elizabeth. I got lucky.

To the Tumblr community, who has followed Alice and Elizabeth since the beginning, leaving encouraging notes and kind words along the way. Even if we've never met, your creativity and openness touched me and touched this story. It took a Tumblr village to raise this book. I'm grateful to each of you for finding *Meditations* in the vast expanse of the Tumblrverse.

Thanks to all my friends who read this book when it was still in its infancy, a college girl's Word document filled with red squiggly lines, many run-on sentences, and my hopes and dreams: Lindsey Hall, Cori Cagide, Eleni Meadows, Brielle Saracini, and Ivan Perilla. You suffered through initial drafts, and, as with our friendship, you stuck with me. I'm eternally grateful. Also, with sincere gratitude to my friends who offered encouragement of Herculean proportions, not because you felt you had to, but because you believed that writing this story was a worthwhile pursuit, even when I became moody or reclusive for long periods of time: Missy Witt, Ana Driggs, Jenna Ham, Liza Semenova, and Marita Provus.

Thank you to Lindsey Hall, a friend who the universe also happened to make my colleague. You helped instill that dialogue is best when direct, simple, and quick. A skill we are still working on mastering in daily life. Your edits and comments were crucial, as was your unwavering encouragement.

This wouldn't be a proper acknowledgment without a nod

to the legendary Lewis Carroll, who is immortalized in his 150-year-old tale of Alice and her eternally expanding Wonderland. He encouraged us to believe in nonsense and in our own imaginations, while reminding us that the former is not the latter.

Deepest gratitude to my parents, Rick and Diane Patrick, who gave me the moments when Elizabeth remembered her strength. For the moments she remembered where she came from, and grew. For Elizabeth's bravery in her journey to the deepest parts of herself. I wouldn't be able to write with the same conviction had you not given the same moments to me. Thank you for encouraging me to write from the time I dragged around my first "novel" in my composition notebook. Thank you for believing in me and my writing before we knew anything would ever come of it. I hope to repay you with eternal love and reverence, and also with unlimited hugs.

To David and Pauline Woldorf, my Nana and Papa, who I will forever love and forever miss. They aren't here to read this book, but they left their mark on each page.

I'm grateful, too, for my extended family, Dick Pease and my late grandmother, Gene, the Patricks, the Harveys, the Woldorfs, and the Constantines, for your bottomless well of love and support.

Cezar—in countless ways, thank you. For endlessly believing in me and loving me, and for being a consistent muse and an extraordinarily rare soul. What else can I say about a man who knows so much of my own inner Wonderland and is still devoted to exploring the labyrinth further? Thank you for being on this life journey with me, I love you.

Anna first fell in love with Alice, like many children do, when she saw the Disney movie as a little girl. When her family visited the Magic Kingdom, she bashfully but persistently chased Alice's doppelganger around with her autograph book.

Anna was born and raised in Northern Virginia. There, she had the best of both worlds, living in the

Photograph by Cezar Constantine, Central Park, Manhattan, New York, November 2014

fulcrum between the nation's capital and the countryside, enjoying both the bustle and the bird's song outside her window. She grew up an only child and learned how to skillfully entertain herself, creating worlds of her own from a very early age.

After graduating from high school with honors, Anna traveled to London, England, where she spent her first semester of college studying abroad. While there, she came across Lewis Carroll's original handwritten manuscript of *Alice's Adventures in Wonderland* at the British Library. She also made a trip to Oxford and trudged around Charles Lutwidge

Dodgson's rain-drenched "City of Dreaming Spires," where Alice's story first came to life.

Anna completed the rest of her undergraduate education in Boston, where she earned a degree in communications from Boston College. She began writing *Meditations in Wonderland* her last semester. What began as the rought draft of a manuscript Anna created for a fiction workshop became a completed novel by the time she graduated in May.

After graduating, she moved to New York City with her boyfriend, Cezar. It was through her job as a book publicist that she made the serendipitous acquaintance of Hobbs Allison from Greenleaf Book Group, who gave this book a loving home.

After two years in New York City, she and Cezar moved back to Northern Virginia and returned to their roots.

This is Anna's first time taking a tumble down the rabbit hole as an author.

Visit www.meditationsinwonderland.com to read more about Anna, this book, and future titles. She can be found across the social media universe at @loveannapatrick.

1. What is the true meaning of "self-love" and "self-acceptance"? Are they the same thing? In what ways are they different? Are they truly attainable, or are our relationships with ourselves ever evolving? Do you think Elizabeth attains either or both?

2. Did you find the tone of Elizabeth's "Wonderland" to be disturbing, whimsical, or frightening? In what ways is the mood of this Wonderland different from that of the original Wonderland? What does that tone say about what's happening beneath Elizabeth's surface?

3. The Cheshire Cat tells Elizabeth: "What better way to find your courage than to look in the deepest, most maddening crevices of the mind!" Do you think Elizabeth is brave? What do we know about her? What emotions motivate her at the beginning of the story compared to the end? What does Elizabeth learn about herself and the world?

4. In what ways are Elizabeth and Alice similar? In what ways are they different? Do those similarities and differences take on a new meaning at the end of the story?

5. Consider the old saying, "We are our own worst enemies." Alice, or "the girl in the blue dress," is an interesting and elusive character—what do we know about her? Who is she and what does she represent? What reaction do the characters in Wonderland have toward her? Do you see her as ultimately bad or good? Do you think she is trying to help Elizabeth, or is she just toying with her?

6. Describe the dynamic between Adam and Elizabeth. What does their apartment reveal about their relationship? How has the past shaped their lives? How does this dynamic change by the end of the novel? What weaknesses and strengths did each of them have? How was their dynamic further unveiled in chapter nine?

7. The author uses a lot of symbolism throughout the story. What are some of these symbols and what do they represent?

8. When Elizabeth finds Alice's first letter, she is told that Wonderland is a representation of her subconscious. What, or whom, do each of the characters in Wonderland represent for Elizabeth, and what do they represent universally? What would your "Wonderland" look like?

9. The author has taken a classic children's story and turned it into a gripping, cerebral piece of adult literature. In what ways is the classic story translated within this one? How have the characters changed in this retelling?

10. What is the role of the Cheshire Cat in the book? How does the Cheshire Cat move the plot along? How does this version of the Cheshire Cat compare to the one from the original story? What does the Cheshire Cat mean to Elizabeth, and how does that compare with what the original Cheshire Cat meant to Alice in the classic story?

11. The characters Doubt and Worry live inside Elizabeth's subconscious. What role do they play in the story? How do they influence the decisions that Elizabeth makes? By the end of the novel, do you think Elizabeth has rid herself of them?

12. There is a fine line between the real world and the fantastical world in this story. What parts of the story do you feel are real? Which parts do you feel take place in Elizabeth's imagination? What do you think the author is suggesting by keeping those lines blurry?

13. Mirrors and mirror images play an important role throughout the text. How are they significant? What do they represent? Are they a positive or negative force throughout the story? Does this change as the story progresses?

14. Elizabeth's struggle to face herself in the mirror preceded her fall down the rabbit hole. Knowing now what she learned in Wonderland, what do you think is the real reason behind this conflict with the mirror? Do you think this conflict is ultimately resolved by the end of the story?

15. In her first meeting with the Cheshire Cat, he tells Elizabeth: "You find silence only in the absence of your mind, where there is Nothing. Not even You." What role does emptiness play in the book? How does Elizabeth cope with the idea of silence and emptiness? Does that change by the end of the novel?

16. What did you think of the twist at the end? What are your thoughts on Elizabeth's world? Is it real? Is it imagined? Could she still be meditating on her yoga mat? Is Elizabeth mad, too?

17. Is this a book about addiction, or about an inward journey to self-acceptance?

18. Having finished the book, why do you think the author chose to introduce *Meditations in Wonderland* with the quote by T.S. Eliot at the beginning of the novel?

AUTHOR Q & A

1. When did you first know that you wanted to write a novel?

I've wondered about that often, and I never truly understood the answer until recently.

First, a little background. Like most writers, I carried the story around in my head until I simply burst, and it grew into this novel. I grew up with a love for reading, which developed into a love for writing. I've been writing for as long as I can remember, from poetry to stories of all genres. I started writing my first "novel" in elementary school. I scribbled it in pencil in a composition notebook that I kept in my backpack. As with that story, this one also chose me. It started with a few observations that coalesced into words, scenes, and chapters.

But the deeper truth came to me when I was reading a passage from Jorge Luis Borges' "Borges and I" for the fiction workshop I took during my senior year of college, the same workshop that shaped this novel. In it, Borges describes a distinct voice that he credits with writing everything he's ever written. The passage ends with, "I am not sure which of us it is that's writing this passage."

I've been compelled by a similar phenomenon, a voice

which urges me to write, feeding me the words only when it's convenient for him—whether that's while I'm sitting at my laptop getting ready to write, or when I'm trying to fall asleep. My muse is an artist and a sadist in that way. Like the voice who wrote this book, my taste runs to *Alice in Wonderland*, labyrinths, witchy vibes, flawed heroes, dark woods, the taste of chai, magical surrealist prose, and the work of Russian writers. I'm thankful to Borges for the grateful reminder that this disembodied writer in residence is something many writers experience—or we're all just crazy. As the Cheshire Cat said in chapter seven, "Po-tay-toe, po-TAH-toe!"

Every day I discover more beautiful, curious, dark, and twisted things, waiting to be unleashed on paper. I'm a vehicle to the narrator inside me that longs to tell those stories—I have come to accept that while I'll probably never tame that voice, with a regular writing and meditation practice I can keep him on a leash.

2. Do you have any unusual or special practices that help you write?

My writing practice has changed a lot since I first started writing this book. It grew with me over time, much as the story itself did. What has remained, though, is visualization and music. When I'm trying to write a character or a scene it helps me to map it out in images, which has subsequently sent me into a spiraling Pinterest addiction from which I will likely never recover. Once I have certain images mapped out, I choose music that matches the tone I want to convey for the scene, or chapter, that I'm writing. I wrote most of this book to the *Anna Karenina* motion picture soundtrack by Dario Marianelli, particularly the song "Unavoidable." The rest was a mix of Nirvana, Filter, Jefferson Airplane, Pink Floyd, and Hans Zimmer songs.

Additional aspects of my writing practice were largely influenced by my fiction writing workshop professor my senior year of college, who gave me invaluable advice: Carry a small Moleskine notebook with you wherever you go, to help you catch those fleeting ideas that come in often inconvenient moments. A lot of ideas for this book came to me while I was walking to classes, as I had a mile walk to and from campus. I filled up two writing this book. I like to make them motivational as well—the first one I was lucky enough to have signed by Karen Russell, who wrote, "Anna! Write on, girl!" (Hi Karen, thanks for the encouragement!) The second one I bought at a street fair in New York City, which has the white rabbit on it, and says, "Wonderland Passport."

3. Who are a few authors who have influenced your writing?

Like most writers, my desire to write first came from a love of reading. Growing up I gravitated toward Lemony Snicket's *Series of Unfortunate Events*, *The Phantom Tollbooth* by Norton Juster, Neil Gaiman's *Coraline*, and I loved Edgar Allan Poe. I welcomed dark, dystopian, and surrealism with open arms. My childhood was idyllic, so I think I liked the contrast, and the ability to explore a radically different world than the one I knew. I was an imaginative observer with messy hair and a faint scent of horsehair and leather soap.

When I was in high school I first discovered the Russian writers, which was a torrid love affair that turned into a lasting romance. Dostoevsky's *Crime and Punishment* and *The Brothers Karamazov* were life-changing reads for me. As was *Speak, Memory* and many pieces by Vladimir Nabokov. I read Bulgakov's *The Master and Margarita* in translation in a Russian literature class that I took during my senior year of college while I wrote this novel, and it informed many aspects of my writing.

A few others bear mentioning as well. *Heart of Darkness* by Joseph Conrad is one of the only books I've re-read in my life—I think I've read it three or four times and likely will again. *The Road* by Cormac McCarthy, *In Cold Blood* by Truman Capote, and George Orwell's *1984*. Of course, it goes without saying, Lewis Carroll's works.

All of those writers and books left invisible fingerprints on this book in their own ways.

4. Did you have the plot developed to the end, or did the novel unfold in terms of plot as you wrote it?

I started with a general outline, which fell into the thirteen chapters still encapsulated here. There were some symbolic scenes that I had always had in my mind, like the confrontation between Alice and Elizabeth in Alice's house of mirrors. When it came to individual scenes, I let them unfold naturally. Like she did for Elizabeth, Alice left me clues along the way that let me know where she wanted to go next.

5. What inspired you to write a novel based on the classic Alice in Wonderland?

I think Alice touches every person who has ever visited her world. Like many children, Alice has been a love of mine since I was a little girl and first saw the Disney version of *Alice in Wonderland*. I grew up watching that and various film and TV remakes, as well as reading Lewis Carroll's original works. I loved the song "In a World of My Own," maybe because I was an only child and had an overactive imagination. I grew up riding horses and spending a lot of time out in nature, particularly in the woods, so I felt like Wonderland was a very real place. Alice came back to me on and off during my young adulthood.

My freshman year of college, three years before I started writing this novel, I studied abroad in London and saw Carroll's original handwritten manuscript of *Alice's Adventures in Wonderland* on display at the British Library. At one point I found myself alone in the room, just it and me. I was mesmerized by it, held captive where I stood—it felt like a big moment, though I wasn't sure why. A few months later I traveled to Oxford with my classmates, and took a tour of Carroll's stomping grounds, listening to tales of the "real" Alice and other characters, like the shopkeeper that inspired the Sheep in *Through the Looking-Glass*. I loved seeing his world and imagining the ways in which it mirrored Wonderland and the stories he wrote that I loved so much.

The seeds that were sown up to that point began to take root my senior year at Boston College, when I wrote this novel. From the first time I sat down to write the outline it poured out of me, the words were irrepressible. I wrote it in order, page by page in succession. Five months later I had a completed manuscript.

It was a happy coincidence that this book published right around the 150th anniversary of the original publication of *Alice's Adventures in Wonderland*. When I finished writing the original draft of this story I graduated with the sesquicentennial class at Boston College, and I am honored to offer this book as a celebration of Alice's sesquicentennial anniversary.

6. *Can you tell us more about the character Elizabeth and why she feels so disconnected at the beginning of the book?*

I think Elizabeth represents someone who by all societal metrics for success is doing just fine on the surface—she's supporting herself, has a full-time job and a serious relationship—but she has completely disconnected from herself, and that has left her body busy but her soul thirsty. On paper she has it all, but in reality she doesn't feel truly happy despite that, and she's not sure why. She comes to realize that it's because she lost herself somewhere along the way, and that getting in touch with herself again also means reconciling some of the darker parts of herself that she felt more content avoiding for so long.

I think that process is a regular part of the human condition. When we get caught up in going through the motions of life, of not dealing with certain things that have a hold on us, we start to create this sense of disconnect that leaves us feeling lost, uneasy, and unaware of who we really are and what we want. At that point life turns into a labyrinth of choices—we follow the maze without asking ourselves where we're truly going and why.

All of that rings true for Elizabeth, who I consider to be a flawed hero on an internal hero's journey, by Joseph Campbell's paradigm. You get the feeling that everything she has ever let go of has claw marks on it. By refusing to revisit painful events from her past she has fragmented herself to the point of being at the mercy of the voices in her head, which don't feel like her own, that make her question herself. She reaches a point where she can't quiet those internal calls to action anymore, with prescription medication or with meditation. That moment of surrender leads her to her internal search and exploration—and, ultimately, healing and reunification of the self.

7. *Did you base any of the characters in* Meditations in Wonderland *on your real-life experiences?*

Before I answer this I want to make a disclaimer: whether something is based on real life or not is not to say that just because something wasn't real doesn't mean that it is somehow less relevant. In short, the answer to this questions lives in a gray area. While most of this story was derived from observation and imagination, there are times when imagination, such as in dreams, is just as real as a real-life experience.

I have a lot of dreams where I'm wandering through the woods. I took some writing inspiration from those experiences, and it is also worth noting that much of the words in this story came to me in dreams, from a stark writing desk in an undisclosed location in my subconscious mind.

Dreams and subconscious aside, any other parallels to real life within this book were garnered from observation. I likely couldn't have written this story if I hadn't spent so much time in the woods and out in nature over the years. Regarding the urban setting, I did live with my boyfriend in New York City for two years in a studio apartment, though for the majority of the time while this book was being written we lived in Boston, where I pursued my undergraduate degree at Boston College. I did have an orange cat growing up, though, to my knowledge, he didn't possess any of the Cheshire Cat's supernatural qualities.

With all of that said, *Meditations* is a work of fiction. I've never struggled with prescription drug abuse. My relationship is in many ways different than Elizabeth and Adam's. My own inner "Wonderland" would look much different than the one presented here, as it would for any other individual reading this.

A famous actor once said that we love to play the characters that are the opposite of what we perceive ourselves to be. I like to write characters and relationships that are the foil of what I perceive many real-life people and relationships that I have observed to be—that's the joy and essence of fiction, after all.

I also owe a large debt of inspiration to Lewis Carroll for his original work of fiction.

8. *Which character in* Meditations in Wonderland *do you personally identify with and why?*

I think I can find a little bit of myself in all of them. I identify with Elizabeth in the moments when I feel lost or delicate, in the moments when I remind myself that I'm strong, and when I allow myself to feel both at the same time. I see myself in Alice when I'm hard on myself, but also in those moments when I push myself to look deeper, and when I accept and embrace myself with all of my flaws and strengths. I feel like the Cheshire Cat when I laugh at the little moments that often go unnoticed, and when I become mindful of my path and remember to enjoy it along my way. I relate to Adam when he tries to use his compassion to help the ones he loves the most, even in his own understated ways. I connect with the animals in the meadow courtyard, when I find myself unconsciously rambling on and on . . .

9. *Which was your favorite scene to write in* Meditations in Wonderland*?*

My favorite scene to write would have to be the confrontation between Elizabeth and Alice in chapter twelve, specifically the moment when Elizabeth watches her journey play back in the mirror and so much comes to light. With any hero's journey, especially an inner journey, the moment of epiphany is a sacred moment—a moment where the flawed hero is more than her insecurities, more than her shortcomings and problems, and more than the challenges she faced to get to where she now stands. In that moment she's an enlightened hero, fully herself, the master of her fate. There is an element of silent knowing, magic, and intimacy to that moment that I love, Elizabeth and Alice become the witches conjuring a profound awakening that we experience along with them, making it a special moment for the writer and reader, as well as a reward for the journey.

Another one of my favorite scenes to write was from chapter seven, when Tweedle Dee and Tweedle Dum face off with one another. It was a whimsical break from the darkness, and I think we all cherish those moments.

10. *Who is your favorite character in* Meditations in Wonderland *and why?*

Alice. She's nothing if not raw and honest. She's that voice inside all of us that keeps us on our toes. The voice that can be cruel, but pushes us forward. The voice that refuses to be silenced, the beast that refuses to be put back in its cage. And who doesn't love a good villain?

11. *Are you currently working on another novel? And, if so, can you tell us a bit about it?*

Both the good and the bad thing about having an internal narrator is that he never sleeps—there are always more novels waiting to be written. There are two or three that I am most interested in, and that includes a potential sequel where Elizabeth and Alice battle it out in the real world. *Through the Looking-Glass* was the sequel to *Alice's Adventures in Wonderland*, so there may be some inspired elements there. The pieces are already falling into place in a similar manner as they did with this book. I'll let my unfettered muse lead the way.

12. *What would you say to those struggling on the journey to find themselves?*

Allow yourself to explore your own inner Wonderland, and let yourself be rattled and riveted by it. Be curious, meditate, read, think. Go to the places that scare you, and bring a flashlight. Smile at the monsters, blow kisses at them. Remember that you're the one looking into the mirror, and you're the one looking back. Take every step of your journey with love. Embrace your inner Alice—love her, but always keep her on a leash.

CPSIA information can be obtained
at www.ICGtesting.com
Printed in the USA
LVOW11s1735091217
559215LV00004B/645/P